El

Winner of the
Nebula Award
World Fantasy Award
Tiptree Award
Shirley Jackson Award
Mythopoeic Award

"Hand is an expert at building mood and atmosphere in ways that you don't realize until you feel it around you."
—*SF Signal*

"A predilection for probing the translucent borderline between magic and reality . . . a beautifully nuanced, often disquieting style."
—*Booklist*

"Fiercely frightening yet hauntingly beautiful."
—Tess Gerritsen, author of *Playing with Fire* and the Rizzoli and Isles series

"Quite simply one of our best living writers."
—Nick Antosca, author of *The Girlfriend Game*

"Hand does for upstate New York what Stephen King has done for rural Maine."
—*Publishers Weekly*

PM PRESS OUTSPOKEN AUTHORS SERIES

1. *The Left Left Behind*
   Terry Bisson

2. *The Lucky Strike*
   Kim Stanley Robinson

3. *The Underbelly*
   Gary Phillips

4. *Mammoths of the Great Plains*
   Eleanor Arnason

5. *Modem Times 2.0*
   Michael Moorcock

6. *The Wild Girls*
   Ursula K. Le Guin

7. *Surfing the Gnarl*
   Rudy Rucker

8. *The Great Big Beautiful Tomorrow*
   Cory Doctorow

9. *Report from Planet Midnight*
   Nalo Hopkinson

10. *The Human Front*
    Ken MacLeod

11. *New Taboos*
    John Shirley

12. *The Science of Herself*
    Karen Joy Fowler

PM PRESS OUTSPOKEN AUTHORS SERIES

13. *Raising Hell*
Norman Spinrad

14. *Patty Hearst & The Twinkie Murders: A Tale of Two Trials*
Paul Krassner

15. *My Life, My Body*
Marge Piercy

16. *Gypsy*
Carter Scholz

17. *Miracles Ain't What They Used to Be*
Joe R. Lansdale

18. *Fire.*
Elizabeth Hand

Fire.

plus

"The Saffron Gatherers"

and

"Beyond Belief: On Becoming a Writer"

and

"Flying Squirrels in the Rafters"
Outspoken Interview

and

much more

Elizabeth Hand

PM PRESS | 2017

"Tom Disch" was originally published as "Remembering Thomas M. Disch," *Salon*, July 11, 2008.
"Beyond Belief" was originally published as "The Profession of Science Fiction, 59: Beyond Belief," in *Foundation* 90 (Spring 2004).
"The Woman Men Didn't See" is adapted by the author from a book review, "Go Ask Alice," in *Fantasy & Science Fiction* 111 (October–November 2006).
"Kronia" and "The Saffron Gatherers" are both from the author's collection *Saffron and Brimstone: Strange Stories* (Milwaukie, OR: M Press, 2006).
"Fire." is original to this volume.

Fire.

Series editor: Terry Bisson

ISBN: 978-1-62963-234-6
Library of Congress Control Number: 2016948150

Outsides: John Yates/Stealworks.com
Author photograph: Liza Trombi/Locus Publications
Insides: Jonathan Rowland

PM Press
P.O. Box 23912
Oakland, CA 94623
www.pmpress.org

10 9 8 7 6 5 4 3 2 1

Printed in the USA by the Employee Owners of Thomson-Shore in Dexter, Michigan
www.thomsonshore.com

CONTENTS

The Saffron Gatherers

He had almost been as much a place to her as a person; the lost domain, the land of heart's desire. Alone at night she would think of him as others might imagine an empty beach, blue water; for years she had done this, and fallen into sleep.

She flew to Seattle to attend a symposium on the Future. It was a welcome trip—on the East Coast, where she lived, it had rained without stopping for thirty-four days. A meteorological record, now a tired joke: only six more days to go! Even Seattle was drier than that.

She was part of a panel discussion on natural disasters and global warming. Her first three novels had presented near-future visions of apocalypse; she had stopped writing them when it became less like fiction and too much like reportage. Since then she had produced a series of time-travel books, wish-fulfillment fantasies about visiting the ancient world. Many of her friends and colleagues in the field had turned to similar themes, retro, nostalgic, historical. Her academic background was in classical archeology; the research was joyous, if exhausting. She hated to fly, the constant round of threats and delay.

The weather and concomitant poverty, starvation, drought, flooding, riots—it had all become so bad that it was like an extreme sport now, to visit places that had once unfolded from one's imagination in the brightly colored panoramas of 1920s postal cards. Still she went, armed with eyeshade, earplugs, music, and pills that put her to sleep. Behind her eyes, she saw Randall's arm flung above his head, his face half-turned from hers on the pillow. Fifteen minutes after the panel had ended she was in a cab on her way to SeaTac. Several hours later she was in San Francisco.

He met her at the airport. After the weeks of rain back East and Seattle's muted sheen, the sunlight felt like something alive, clawing at her eyes. They drove to her hotel, the same place she always stayed; like something from an old B-movie, the lobby with its ornate cast-iron stair-rail, the narrow front desk of polished walnut; clerks who all might have been played by the young Peter Lorre. The elevator with its illuminated dial like a clock that could never settle on the time; an espresso shop tucked into the back entrance, no bigger than a broom closet.

Randall always had to stoop to enter the elevator. He was very tall, not as thin as he had been when they first met, nearly twenty years earlier. His hair was still so straight and fine that it always felt wet, but the luster had faded from it: it was no longer dark-blond but grey, a strange dusky color, almost blue in some lights, like pale damp slate. He had grey-blue eyes; a habit of looking up through downturned black lashes that at first had seemed coquettish. She had since learned it was part of a deep reticence, a detachment from the world that sometimes seemed to border on the pathological. You might call him an agoraphobe, if he had stayed indoors.

But he didn't. They had grown up in neighboring towns in New York, though they only met years later, in DC. When the time came to choose allegiance to a place, she fled to Maine, with all those other writers and artists seeking a retreat into the past; he chose Northern California. He was a journalist, a staff writer for a glossy magazine that only came out four times a year, each issue costing as much as a bottle of decent sémillon. He interviewed scientists engaged in paradigm-breaking research, Nobel Prize–winning writers; poets who wrote on their own skin and had expensive addictions to drugs that subtly altered their personalities, the tenor of their words, so that each new book or online publication seemed to have been written by another person. Multiple Poets' Disorder, Randall had tagged this, and the term stuck; he was the sort of writer who coined phrases. He had a curved mouth, beautiful long fingers. Each time he used a pen, she was surprised again to recall that he was left-handed. He collected incunabula—*Ars oratoria*, Jacobus Publicius's disquisition on the art of memory; the *Opera Philosophica* of Seneca, containing the first written account of an earthquake; Pico della Mirandola's *Heptaplus*—as well as manuscripts. His apartment was filled with quarter-sawn oaken barrister's bookcases, glass fronts bright as mirrors, holding manuscript binders, typescripts, wads of foolscap bound in leather. By the window overlooking the Bay, a beautiful old mapchest of letters written by Neruda, Beckett, Asaré. There were signed broadsheets on the walls, and drawings, most of them inscribed to Randall. He was two years younger than she was. Like her, he had no children. In the years since his divorce, she had never heard him mention his former wife by name.

The hotel room was small and stuffy. There was a wooden ceiling fan that turned slowly, barely stirring the white curtain that covered the single window. It overlooked an airshaft. Directly across was another old building, a window that showed a family sitting at a kitchen table, eating beneath a fluorescent bulb.

"Come here, Suzanne," said Randall. "I have something for you."

She turned. He was sitting on the bed—a nice bed, good mattress and expensive white linens and duvet—reaching for the leather mailbag he always carried to remove a flat parcel.

"Here," he said. "For you."

It was a book. With Randall it was always books. Or expensive tea: tiny, neon-colored foil packets that hissed when she opened them and exuded fragrances she could not describe, dried leaves that looked like mouse droppings, or flower petals, or fur; leaves that, once infused, tasted of old leather and made her dream of complicated sex.

"Thank you," she said, unfolding the mauve tissue the book was wrapped in. Then, as she saw what it was, "Oh! Thank you!"

"Since you're going back to Thera. Something to read on the plane."

It was an oversized book in a slipcase: the classic edition of *The Thera Frescoes*, by Nicholas Spirotiadis, a volume that had been expensive when first published, twenty years earlier. Now it must be worth a fortune, with its glossy thick photographic paper and fold-out pages depicting the larger murals. The slip-case art was a detail from the site's most famous image, the painting known as *The Saffron Gatherers*. It showed the profile of a beautiful young woman dressed in an elaborately patterned tiered skirt and blouse, her head shaven save for a serpentine coil of dark hair, her brow tattooed. She wore hoop earrings and bracelets, two on her right hand, one on her left. Bell-like tassels hung from her sleeves. She was plucking the stigma from a crocus blossom. Her fingernails were painted red.

Suzanne had seen the original painting a decade ago, when it was easier for American researchers to gain access to the restored ruins and the National Archaeological Museum in Athens. After two years of paperwork and bureaucratic wheedling, she had just received permission to return.

"It's beautiful," she said. It still took her breath away, how modern the girl looked, not just her clothes and jewelry and body art but her expression, lips parted, her gaze at once imploring and vacant: the fifteen-year-old who had inherited the earth.

"Well, don't drop it in the tub." Randall leaned over to kiss her head. "That was the only copy I could find on the net. It's become a very scarce book."

"Of course," said Suzanne, and smiled.

"Claude is going to meet us for dinner. But not till seven. Come here—"

They lay in the dark room. His skin tasted of salt and bitter lemon; his hair against her thighs felt warm, liquid. She shut her eyes and imagined him beside her, his long limbs and rueful mouth; opened her eyes and there he was, now, sleeping. She held her hand above his chest and felt heat radiating from him, a scent like honey. She began to cry silently.

His hands. That big rumpled bed. In two days she would be gone, the room would be cleaned. There would be nothing to show she had ever been here at all.

***

They drove to an Afghan restaurant in North Beach. Randall's car was older, a second-generation hybrid; even with the grants and tax breaks, a far more expensive vehicle than she or anyone she knew back East could ever afford. She had never gotten used to how quiet it was.

Outside, the sidewalks were filled with people, the early evening light silvery-blue and gold, like a sun shower. Couples arm-in-arm, children, groups of students waving their hands as they spoke on their cell phones, a skateboarder hustling to keep up with a pack of parkour practitioners.

"Everyone just seems so much more absorbed here," she said. Even the panhandlers were antic.

"It's the light. It makes everyone happy. Also the drugs they put in our drinking water." She laughed, and he put his arm around her.

Claude was sitting in the restaurant when they arrived. He was a poet who had gained notoriety and then prominence in the late 1980s with the *Hyacinthus Elegies*, his response to the AIDS epidemic. Randall first interviewed him after Claude received his MacArthur Fellowship. They subsequently became good friends. On the wall of his flat, Randall had a hand-written copy of the second elegy, with one of the poet's signature drawings of a hyacinth at the bottom.

"Suzanne!" He jumped up to embrace her, shook hands with Randall, then beckoned them both to sit. "I ordered some wine. A good cab I heard about from someone at the gym."

Suzanne adored Claude. The day before she left for Seattle, he'd sent flowers to her, a half-dozen delicate *Narcissus serotinus*, with long white narrow petals and tiny yellow throats. Their sweet scent perfumed her entire small house. She'd e-mailed him profuse but also wistful thanks—they were such an extravagance, and so lovely; and she had to leave before she could enjoy them fully. He was a few years younger than she was, thin and muscular, his face and skull hairless save for a wispy black beard. He had lost his eyebrows during a round of chemo and had feathery lines, like antennae, tattooed in their place and threaded with gold beads. His chest and arms were heavily tattooed with stylized flowers, dolphins, octopi, the same iconography Suzanne had seen in Akrotiri and Crete; and also with the names of lovers and friends and colleagues who had died. Along the inside of his arms you could still see the stippled marks left by hypodermic needles—they looked like tiny black beads worked into the pattern of waves and swallows and the faint white traces of an adolescent suicide attempt. His expression was gentle and melancholy, the face of a tired ascetic, or a benign Antonin Artaud.

"I should have brought the book!" Suzanne sat beside him, shaking her head in dismay. "This beautiful book that Randall gave me—Spirotiadis' Thera book?"

"No! I've heard of it, I could never find it. Is it wonderful?"

"It's gorgeous. You would love it, Claude."

They ate, and spoke of his collected poetry, forthcoming next winter; of Suzanne's trip to Akrotiri. Of Randall's next interview, with a woman on the House Committee on Bioethics who was rumored to be sympathetic to the pro-cloning lobby, but only in cases involving "only" children—no siblings, no twins or multiples—who died before age fourteen.

"Grim," said Claude. He shook his head and reached for the second bottle of wine. "I can't imagine it. Even pets . . ."

He shuddered, then turned to rest a hand on Suzanne's shoulder. "So: back to Santorini. Are you excited?"

"I am. Just seeing that book, it made me excited again. It's such an incredible place—you're there, and you think, What could this have been? If it had survived, if it all hadn't just gone *bam*, like that—"

"Well, then it would really have gone," said Randall." I mean, it would have been lost. There would have been no volcanic ash to preserve it. All your paintings, we would never have known them. Just like we don't know anything else from back then."

"We know some things," said Suzanne. She tried not to sound annoyed—there was a lot of wine, and she was jet-lagged. "Plato. Homer . . ."

"Oh, them," said Claude, and they all laughed. "But he's right. It would all have turned to dust by now. All rotted away. All one with Baby Jesus, or Baby Zeus. Everything you love would be buried under a Tradewinds Resort. Or it would be like Athens, which would be even worse."

"Would it?" She sipped her wine. "We don't know that. We don't know what it would have become. This—"

She gestured at the room, the couple sitting beneath twinkling rose-colored lights, playing with a digital toy that left little chattering faces in the air as the woman switched it on and off. Outside, dusk and neon. "It might have become like this."

"This." Randall leaned back in his chair, staring at her. "Is this so wonderful?"

"Oh yes," she said, staring back at him, the two of them unsmiling. "This is all a miracle."

He excused himself. Claude refilled his glass and turned back to Suzanne. "So. How are things?"

"With Randall?" She sighed. "It's good. I dunno. Maybe it's great. Tomorrow—we're going to look at houses."

Claude raised a tattooed eyebrow "Really?"

She nodded. Randall had been looking at houses for three years now, ever since the divorce.

"Who knows?" she said. "Maybe this will be the charm. How hard can it be to buy a house?"

"In San Francisco? Doll, it's easier to win the stem cell lottery. But yes, Randall is a very discerning buyer. He's the last of the true idealists. He's looking for the eidos of the house. Plato's eidos; not Socrates'," he added. "Is this the first time you've gone looking with him?"

She managed another nod, almost a shrug; was it?

"Well. Maybe that is great," he said. "Or not. Would you move out here?"

"I don't know. Maybe. If he had a house. Probably not."

"Why?"

"I don't know. I guess I'm looking for the eidos of something else. Out here, it's just too . . ."

She opened her hands as though catching rain. Claude looked at her quizzically.

"Too sunny?" he said. "Too warm? Too beautiful?"

"I suppose. The land of the lotus-eaters. I love knowing it's here, but." She drank more wine. "Maybe if I had more job security."

"You're a writer. It's against nature for you to have job security."

"Yeah, no kidding. What about you? You don't ever worry about that?"

He gave her his sweet sad smile and shook his head. "Never. The world will always need poets. We're like the lilies of the field."

"What about journalists?" Randall appeared behind them, slipping his cell phone back into his pocket. "What are we?"

"Quackgrass," said Claude.

"Cactus," said Suzanne.

"Oh, gee. I get it," said Randall. "Because we're all hard and spiny and no one loves us."

"Because you only bloom once a year," said Suzanne.

"When it rains," added Claude.

"That was my realtor." Randall sat and downed the rest of his wine. "Sunday's open house day. Two o'clock till four. Suzanne, we have a lot of ground to cover."

He gestured for the waiter. Suzanne leaned over to kiss Claude's cheek.

"When do you leave for Hydra?" she asked.

"Tomorrow."

"Tomorrow!" She looked crestfallen. "That's so soon!"

"The beautiful life was brief," said Claude, and laughed. "You're only here till Monday. I have a reservation on the ferry from Piraeus, I couldn't change it."

"How long will you be there? I'll be in Athens Tuesday after next, then I go to Akrotiri."

Claude smiled. "That might work. Here—"

He copied out a phone number in his careful, calligraphic hand.

"This is Zali's number on Hydra. A cell phone, I have no idea if it will even work. But I'll see you soon. Like you said—"

He lifted his thin hands and gestured at the room around them, his dark eyes wide. "This is a miracle."

Randall paid the check and they turned to go. At the door, Claude hugged Suzanne. "Don't miss your plane," he said.

"Don't wind her up!" said Randall.

"Don't miss yours," said Suzanne. Her eyes filled with tears as she pressed her face against Claude's. "It was so good to see you. If I miss you, have a wonderful time in Hydra."

"Oh, I will," said Claude. "I always do."

***

Randall dropped her off at her hotel. She knew better than to ask him to stay; besides, she was tired, and the wine was starting to give her a headache.

"Tomorrow," he said. "Nine o'clock. A leisurely breakfast, and then . . ."

He leaned over to open her door, then kissed her. "The exciting new world of California real estate?"

Outside, the evening had grown cool, but the hotel room still felt close: it smelled of sex, and the sweetish dusty scent of old books. She opened the window by the airshaft and went to take a shower. Afterwards she got into bed, but found herself unable to sleep.

The wine, she thought; always a mistake. She considered taking one of the anti-anxiety drugs she carried for flying, but decided against it. Instead she picked up the book Randall had given her.

She knew all the images, from other books and websites, and the island itself. Nearly four thousand years ago, now; much of it might have been built yesterday. Beneath fifteen feet of volcanic ash and pumice, homes with ocean views and indoor plumbing, pipes that might have channeled steam from underground vents fed by the volcano the city was built upon. Fragments of glass that might have been windows, or lenses. The great pithoi that still held food when they were opened millennia later. Great containers of honey for trade, for embalming the Egyptian dead. Yellow grains of pollen. Wine.

But no human remains. No bones, no grimacing tormented figures as were found beneath the sand at Herculaneum, where the fishermen had fled and died. Not even animal remains, save for the charred vertebrae of a single donkey. They had all known to leave. And when they did, their city was not abandoned in frantic haste or fear. All was orderly, the pithoi still sealed, no metal utensils or weapons strewn upon the floor, no bolts of silk or linen; no jewelry.

Only the paintings, and they were everywhere; so lovely and beautifully wrought that at first the excavators thought they had uncovered a temple complex.

But they weren't temples: they were homes. Someone had paid an artist, or teams of artists, to paint frescoes on the walls of room after room after room. Sea daffodils, swallows; dolphins and pleasure boats, the boats themselves decorated with more dolphins and flying seabirds, golden nautilus on their prows. Wreaths of flowers. A shipwreck. Always you saw the same colors, ochre-yellow and ferrous red; a pigment made by grinding glaucophane, a vitreous mineral that produced a grey-blue shimmer; a bright pure French blue. But of course it wasn't French blue but Egyptian blue—Pompeian blue—one of the earliest pigments, used for thousands of years; you made it by combining a calcium compound with ground malachite and quartz, then heating it to extreme temperatures.

But no green. It was a blue and gold and red world. Not even the plants were green.

Otherwise, the paintings were so alive that, when she'd first seen them, she half-expected her finger would be wet if she touched them. The eyes of the boys who played at boxing were children's eyes. The antelopes had the mad topaz glare of wild goats. The monkeys had blue fur and looked like dancing cats. There were people walking in the streets. You could see what their houses looked like, red brick and yellow shutters.

She turned towards the back of the book, to the section on Xeste 3. It was the most famous building at the site. It contained the most famous paintings—the woman known as the "Mistress of Animals." "The Adorants," who appeared to be striding down a fashion runway. "The Lustral Basin."

The saffron gatherers.

She gazed at the image from the East Wall of Room Three, two women harvesting the stigmata of the crocus blossoms. The flowers were like stylized yellow fireworks, growing from the rocks and also appearing in a repetitive motif on the wall above the figures, like the fleur-de-lis patterns on wallpaper. The fragments of painted plaster had been meticulously restored; there was no attempt to fill in what was missing, as had been done at Knossos under Sir Arthur Evans' supervision to sometimes cartoonish effect.

None of that had not been necessary here. The fresco was nearly intact. You could see how the older woman's eyebrow was slightly raised, with annoyance or perhaps just impatience, and count the number of stigmata the younger acolyte held in her outstretched palm.

How long would it have taken for them to fill those baskets? The crocuses bloomed only in autumn, and each small blossom contained just three tiny crimson threads, the female stigmata. It might take 100,000 flowers to produce a half-pound of the spice.

And what did they use the spice for? Cooking; painting; a pigment they traded to the Egyptians for dyeing mummy bandages.

She closed the book. She could hear distant sirens, and a soft hum from the ceiling fan. Tomorrow they would look at houses.

***

For breakfast they went to the Embarcadero, the huge indoor market inside the restored Ferry Building that had been damaged over a century before, in the 1906 earthquake. There was a shop with nothing but olive oil and infused vinegars; another that sold only mushrooms, great woven panniers and baskets filled with tree-ears, portobellos, fungus that looked like orange coral; black morels and matsutake and golden chanterelles.

They stuck with coffee and sweet rolls, and ate outside on a bench looking over the Bay. A man threw sticks into the water for a pair of black labs; another man swam along the embankment. The sunlight was strong and clear as gin, and nearly as potent: it made Suzanne feel lightheaded and slightly drowsy, even though she had just gotten up.

"Now," said Randall. He took out the newspaper, opened it to the real estate section, and handed it to her. He had circled eight listings. "The first two are in Oakland; then we'll hit Berkeley and Kensington. You ready?"

The drove in heavy traffic across the San Francisco–Oakland Bay Bridge. To either side, bronze water that looked as though it would be too hot to swim in; before them the Oakland Hills, where the houses were ranged in undulating lines like waves. Once in the city they began to climb in and out of pocket neighborhoods poised between the arid and the tropic. Bungalows nearly hidden beneath overhanging trees suddenly yielded to bright white stucco houses flanked by aloes and agaves. It looked at once wildly fanciful and comfortable, as though all urban planning had been left to Dr. Seuss.

"They do something here called 'staging,'" said Randall as they pulled behind a line of parked cars on a hillside. A phalanx of realtors' signs rose from a grassy mound beside them. "Homeowners pay thousands and thousands of dollars for a decorator to come in and tart up their houses with rented furniture and art and stuff. So, you know, it looks like it's worth three million dollars."

They walked to the first house, a Craftsman bungalow tucked behind trees like prehistoric ferns. There was a fountain outside, filled with koi that stared up with engorged silvery eyes. Inside, exposed beams and dark hardwood floors so glossy they looked covered with maple syrup. There was a grand piano, and large framed posters from Parisian cafés—Suzanne was to note a lot of these as the afternoon wore on—and much heavy dark Mediterranean-style furniture, as well as a few early Mission pieces that might have been genuine. The kitchen floors were tiled. In the master bath, there were mosaics in the sink and sunken tub.

Randall barely glanced at these. He made a beeline for the deck. After wandering around for a few minutes, Suzanne followed him.

"It's beautiful," she said. Below, terraced gardens gave way to stepped hillsides, and then the city proper, and then the gilded expanse of San Francisco Bay, with sailboats like swans moving slowly beneath the bridge.

"For four million dollars, it better be," said Randall.

She looked at him. His expression was avid, but it was also sad, his pale eyes melancholy in the brilliant sunlight. He drew her to him and gazed out above the treetops, then pointed across the blue water.

"That's where we were. Your hotel, it's right there, somewhere." His voice grew soft. "At night it all looks like a fairy city. The lights, and the bridges . . . You can't believe that anyone could have built it."

He blinked, shading his eyes with his hand, then looked away. When he turned back his cheeks were damp.

"Come on," he said. He bent to kiss her forehead. "Got to keep moving."

They drove to the next house, and the next, and the one after that. The light and heat made her dizzy; and the scents of all the unfamiliar flowers, the play of water in fountains and a swimming pool like a great turquoise lozenge. She found herself wandering through expansive bedrooms with people she did not know, walking in and out of closets, bathrooms, a sauna. Every room seemed lavish, the air charged as though anticipating a wonderful party; tables set with beeswax candles and bottles of wine and crystal stemware. Countertops of hand-thrown Italian tiles; globular cobalt vases filled with sunflowers, another recurring motif.

But there was no sign of anyone who might actually live in one of these houses, only a series of well-dressed women with expensively restrained jewelry who would greet them, usually in the kitchen, and make sure they had a flyer listing the home's attributes. There were plates of cookies, banana bread warm from the oven. Bottles of sparkling water and organic lemonade.

And, always, a view. They didn't look at houses without views. To Suzanne, some were spectacular; others, merely glorious. All were more beautiful than anything she saw from her own windows or deck, where she looked out onto evergreens and grey rocks and, much of the year, snow.

It was all so dreamlike that it was nearly impossible for her to imagine real people living here. For her a house had always meant a refuge from the world; the place where you hid from whatever catastrophe was breaking that morning.

But now she saw that it could be different. She began to understand that, for Randall at least, a house wasn't a retreat. It was a way of engaging with the world; of opening himself to it. The view wasn't yours. You belonged to it, you were a tiny part of it, like the sailboats and the seagulls and the flowers in the garden; like the sunflowers on the highly polished tables.

You were part of what made it real. She had always thought it was the other way around.

"You ready?" Randall came up behind her and put his hand on her neck. "This is it. We're done. Let's go have a drink."

On the way out the door he stopped to talk to the agent. "They'll be taking bids tomorrow," she said. "We'll let you know on Tuesday."

"Tuesday?" Suzanne said in amazement when they got back outside. "You can do all this in two days? Spend a million dollars on a house?"

"Four million," said Randall. "This is how it works out here. The race is to the quick."

She had assumed they would go to another restaurant for drinks and then dinner. Instead, to her surprise, he drove to his flat. He took a bottle of Pommery Louise from the refrigerator and opened it, and she wandered about examining his manuscripts as he made dinner. At the Embarcadero, without her knowing, he had bought chanterelles and morels, imported pasta colored like spring flowers, arugula, and baby tatsoi. For dessert, orange-blossom custard. When they were finished, they remained out on the deck and looked at the Bay, the rented view. Lights shimmered through the dusk. In a flowering quince in the garden, dozens of hummingbirds droned and darted like bees, attacking each other with needle beaks.

"So." Randall's face was slightly flushed. They had finished the champagne, and he had poured them each some cognac. "If this happens—if I get the house. Will you move out here?"

She stared down at the hummingbirds. Her heart was racing. The quince had no smell, none that she could detect, anyway; yet still they swarmed around it. Because it was so large, and its thousands of blossoms were so red. She hesitated, then said, "Yes."

He nodded and took a quick sip of cognac. "Why don't you just stay, then? Till we find out on Tuesday? I have to go down to San Jose early tomorrow to interview this guy, you could come and we could go to that place for lunch."

"I can't." She bit her lip, thinking, "No . . . I wish I could, but I have to finish that piece before I leave for Greece."

"You can't just leave from here?"

"No." That would be impossible, to change her whole itinerary. "And I don't have any of my things—I need to pack, and get my notes . . . I'm sorry."

He took her hand and kissed it. "That's okay. When you get back."

That night she lay in his bed as Randall slept beside her, staring at the manuscripts on their shelves, the framed lines of poetry. His breathing was low, and she pressed her hand against his chest, feeling his ribs beneath the skin, his heartbeat. She thought of canceling her flight; of postponing the entire trip.

But it was impossible. She moved the pillow beneath her head, so that she could see past him, to the wide picture window. Even with the curtains drawn you could see the lights of the city, faraway as stars.

Very early next morning he drove her to the hotel to get her things and then to the airport.

"My cell will be on," he said as he got her bag from the car. "Call me down in San Jose, once you get in."

"I will."

He kissed her and for a long moment they stood at curbside, arms around each other.

"Book your ticket back here," he said at last, and drew away. "I'll talk to you tonight."

She watched him go, the nearly silent car lost among the taxis and limousines; then hurried to catch her flight. Once she had boarded she switched off her cell, then got out her eyemask, earplugs, book, water bottle; she took one of her pills. It took twenty minutes for the drug to kick in, but she had the timing down pat: the plane lifted into the air and she looked out her window, already feeling not so much calm as detached, mildly stoned. It was a beautiful day, cloudless; later it would be hot. As the plane banked above the city she looked down at the skein of roads, cars sliding along them like beads or raindrops on a string. The traffic crept along 280, the road Randall would take to San Jose. She turned her head to keep it in view as the plane leveled out and began to head inland.

Behind her a man gasped; then another. Someone shouted. Everyone turned to look out the windows.

Below, without a sound that she could hear above the jet's roar, the city fell away. Where it met the sea the water turned brown then white then turgid green. A long line of smoke arose—no not smoke, Suzanne thought, starting to rise from her seat; dust. No flames, none that she could see; more like a burning fuse, though there was no fire, nothing but white and brown and black dust, a pall of dust that ran in a straight line from the city's tip north to south, roughly tracking along the interstate. The plane continued to pull away, she had to strain to see it now, a long green line in the water, the bridges trembling and shining like wires. One snapped then fell, another, miraculously, remained intact. She couldn't see the third bridge. Then everything was green crumpled hillsides, vineyards; distant mountains.

People began to scream. The pilot's voice came on, a blaze of static then silence. Then his voice again, not calm but ordering them to remain so. A few passengers tried to clamber into the aisles but flight attendants and other passengers pulled or pushed them back into their seats. She could hear someone getting sick in the front of the plane. A child crying. Weeping, the buzz and bleat of cell phones followed by repeated commands to put them all away.

Amazingly, everyone did. It wasn't a terrorist attack. The plane, apparently, would not plummet from the sky, but everyone was too afraid that it might to turn their phones back on.

She took another pill, frantic, fumbling at the bottle and barely getting the cap back on. She opened it again, put two, no three, pills into her palm and pocketed them. Then she flagged down one of the flight attendants as she rushed down the aisle.

"Here," said Suzanne. The attendant's mouth was wide, as though she were screaming; but she was silent. "You can give these to them—"

Suzanne gestured towards the back of the plane, where a man was repeating the same name over and over and a woman was keening. "You can take one if you want, the dosage is pretty low. Keep them. Keep them."

The flight attendant stared at her. Finally she nodded as Suzanne pressed the pill bottle into her hand.

"Thank you," she said in a low voice. "Thank you so much, I will."

Suzanne watched her gulp one pink tablet, then walk to the rear of the plane. She continued to watch from her seat as the attendant went down the aisle, furtively doling out pills to those who seemed to need them most. After about twenty minutes, Suzanne took another pill. As she drifted into unconsciousness she heard the pilot's voice over the intercom, informing the passengers of what he knew of the disaster. She slept.

The plane touched down in Boston, greatly delayed by the weather, the ripple effect on air traffic from the catastrophe. It had been raining for thirty-seven days. Outside, glass-green sky, the flooded runways and orange cones blown over by the wind. In the plane's cabin the air chimed with the sound of countless cell phones. She called Randall, over and over again; his phone rang but she received no answer, not even his voicemail.

Inside the terminal, a crowd of reporters and television people awaited, shouting questions and turning cameras on them as they stumbled down the corridor. No one ran; everyone found a place to stand, alone, with a cell phone. Suzanne staggered past the news crews, striking at a man who tried to stop her. There were crowds of people around the TV screens, covering their mouths at the destruction. A lingering smell of vomit, of disinfectant. She hurried past them all, lurching slightly, feeling as though she struggled through wet sand. She retrieved her car, joined the endless line of traffic and began the long drive back to that cold green place, trees with leaves that had yet to open though it was already almost June, apple and lilac blossoms rotted brown on their drooping branches.

It was past midnight when she arrived home. The answering machine was blinking. She scrolled through her messages, hands shaking. She listened to just a few words of each, until she reached the last one.

A blast of static, satellite interference; then a voice. It was unmistakably Randall's.

She couldn't make out what he was saying. Everything was garbled, the connection cut out then picked up again. She couldn't tell when he'd called. She played it over again, once, twice, seven times, trying to discern a single word, something in his tone, background noise, other voices; anything to hint when he had called, from where.

It was hopeless. She tried his cell phone again. Nothing.

She stood, exhausted, and crossed the room, touching table, chairs, countertops, like someone on a listing ship. She turned on the kitchen faucet and splashed cold water onto her face. She would go online and begin the process of finding numbers for hospitals, the Red Cross. He could be alive.

She went to her desk to turn on her computer. Beside it, in a vase, were the flowers Claude had sent her, a half-dozen dead narcissus smelling of rank water and slime. Their white petals were wilted, and the color had drained from the pale yellow cups.

All save one. A stem with a furled bloom no bigger than her pinkie, it had not yet opened when she'd left. Now the petals had spread like feathers, revealing its tiny yellow throat, three long crimson threads. She extended her hand to stroke first one stigma, then the next, until she had touched all three; lifted her hand to gaze at her fingertips, golden with pollen, and then at the darkened window. The empty sky, starless. Beneath blue water, the lost world.

Fire.

Everybody gather round. Hold hands. Whose turn is it?

Mine? Okay.

So a poet, a fireman, a director, and a magician all walk into a bar.

Okay, obviously I know this is not a bar. I'm changing some of the details cause it's my turn to tell our story, okay? I know that. We all know that. It's just, that's how a lot of stories start, people walking into a bar. Jokes.

I know, none of this is funny, but what else are we going to do? Food's gone, enough water for what, another day? If we all just take sips. Can people even live on such a small amount of water? With the fire just . . .

I know, right, I'll stop. Back to the story. Five random people walk into a bar. A couple of them know each other from the hiking trail or before. The poet, she had a book won some prize, I can't remember the name. I know, it's sweet. She's an amazing cook, too, that's her day job, she's a chef in this great place in Telluride. And it's actually a firefighter, not a fireman. Definitely not a fire*man*. *She* is a firefighter, we all know what a badass, right? Right! Like would we even have survived here for the last three days without her?

Yeah, I know. Really, thank you, Marina.

Please don't everyone start to cry—*lo siento*, please, I'm sorry, I'm sorry. Can I just start over?

So they all walk into a bar, only it's not a bar. There's a standup comic too, and a rocket scientist. Cause like how great is that, you know how everyone always says "I'm not a rocket scientist"? He *is* a rocket scientist! Robert, how's that imaginary escape pod coming? The imaginary flame-retardant one that'll fly us all back to Denver or wherever the hell they said people would be safe?

Okay, I get it. Also not funny. You're killing me. Talk about a tough crowd.

So a poet, a firefighter, a nuclear physicist guy, a director—right, a documentarian, not a regular filmmaker—and an illusionist, and a standup comic all walk into a bar. Whew! Got one right. They're all on a hike, they all started off before the fire got out of control and became a, whatever they call it.

Right—a megafire. Thanks, Marina.

So they're on a hike and like a thousand other idiots—ten thousand, a hundred thousand, I don't know how many—they're outside and get cut off by the fire. The mega—

Yeah, okay. *The fire event.* I'm fine with calling it that, Lula. Fire event, very nice. That's why it's good to have a poet. They're hiking, though they didn't all start out together, they just end up in the same place.

But not the firefighter, she's not hiking. She's working here. And no, it's not a bar, I think we can all agree on that.

It's a fire tower and a fire research station on top of Mount Reynolds, ten thousand five hundred and forty-seven feet—is that above sea level? I never get that, like do we measure from the beach somewhere a thousand miles away or from the ground up?

All I know is, it was a fucking hike to get here. I've never been so exhausted in my life, and I was on a whole season of *Who Wants to Marry My Mom?* If that show had worked out, probably I wouldn't be here now. Maybe I wouldn't have gone on that stupid retreat in the middle of the woods in the middle of fucking nowhere, Colorado. Maybe things would have been better, maybe not. These days, *quién sabe*?

No, I absolutely would not be here now. I'd be back East with Reuben and Peter and Lou, I'd be with my kids, my family . . .

Lo siento, sorry. You are my family now, I know that. We all know that. *Lo siento*. Just so hard, you know? To . . .

All right, if you're my family—who gets to be Uncle Al?

Yo, thanks, Jeff. Didn't know there was any of that left. Who here thought we'd be having whatever they call it, communion with Jim Beam, when the water ran out? When the water *almost* ran out. Jeff, you're recording all this, right?

I can't say it enough, Jeff really is a genius. When we were hiking up here I thought he was crazy, half the filmmakers I know, they're all about big cameras and shit, big crews. Not Jeff. Just the smartphone, but a fuckload more backup chargers than I've ever seen. We passed Lula and Hermanos on the trail, if I'd known she was a cook—*and a poet!*—and he was a magician I would have stuck with them. In case, you know, she might have made us Thanksgiving dinner and he could have teleported us all somewhere to eat it. Turkey and pecan pie, what I wouldn't—

Right, yeah, sorry again. No food talk. But remember the first day we were up here—I can say this, right?—remember the first day, those lights in the sky? They were so beautiful and scary, me and Marina saw them and I'll admit, I was scared. I thought it was some kind of drones. Bad drones, the kind the terrorists used to start the fires. But I was hoping maybe they were the other kind, the ones they used to fight the LA megafire last year. They worked then, right? I thought maybe they were sending them here. But Marina said no, she'd trained in using them. This must be another kind of drone. So I was kind of nervous, yeah, I was scared.

Then it turns out it wasn't drones but birds, that whole flock of birds on fire—hundreds and hundreds. I know everybody saw them, once they got close. Jeff got that amazing footage. That noise.

And it was horrible when they came down. That smell. But we ate, right? I'm not talking about food here, I'm talking about something else—

I don't know what I'm talking about. Just, birds on fire from the sky. And we at least got to eat. You'd think there'd be all kinds of animals ran up here the way we did, to escape. Like that scene in *Bambi*, remember that? Scared the shit out of me when I was a kid. But at least we could've eaten them.

Jeff, any more of that? Just a—

Thanks. If nothing else, it's good to be someplace where bourbon is a major food group.

So Jeff thought the smoke was getting worse before I did, when we were first hiking here, I mean. We left before dawn, just taking a hike. It seemed like a good idea, why we were here. I saw the news, they said it was far away, or it seemed far away, just not that far away, I guess, or not far enough away. A different state, maybe. I thought the smoke might have drifted from somewhere else, another one of those places where everyone wants to live. Or used to. The mountains, the desert, it's so beautiful. Who wouldn't want to live here, right? Or at least visit. Do your poet magician movie thing. Your nuclear physicist thing. Second home, whatever.

Yeah, you all get it. I know you all get it. Actually, I smelled it first, even before Jeff noticed it. I even said something about no smoking on the trail, no cigarettes or campfires—even I knew about that. I don't smoke anyway, and I've never started a campfire in my life.

But the smell. It was crazy. You all remember it, right? Lula, how did you describe it yesterday when it was your turn?

Like smoke exhaling itself, thrice burnt—that's good, Lula. Why you're the poet.

After a while, I didn't even notice I was breathing it in. But I couldn't smell anything else. I think all the receptors in my nostrils got burned out by the smoke. Which, being around Jeff three days with no bathing facilities, is not such a bad thing.

Yeah bra, I love you too.

I know the smoke thing's different for people with asthma, Hermanos. I wasn't forgetting that. But the respirator helps, right? I wish there were enough for everyone but it's good to take turns. Everyone takes turns with whatever's left. Which isn't much.

No, I won't shut up about it. I'm not done yet. This is *my* version of the story. This is why it's great we have different people ended up here. People from the artist colony, Lula and Hermanos. Hermanos, it's incredible what you're doing. Have you guys seen it? You really have to—Marina, is it okay if we open the safe room and go down? Right now? Cause I don't think everyone has seen it, just me and Marina and him. Would that be okay with you, Hermanos? Marina? Yeah? That would be amazing! Thanks, Marina!

Just everyone be really careful going down the stairs. It's cooler here, even with the A/C dead. Concrete bunker. Also, this is why it's good to have the rocket scientist around, to handle those solar panels if we ever—

Yeah, well, I know there's not enough sun because of the smoke. And I know the light batteries are almost dead. I thought we weren't going to discuss that now. Plus it's my turn, and I definitely do not want to discuss it.

So it's kind of dark down here and I know we can't waste the batteries or the lanterns. But. I think we should see what Hermanos did with his turn. Cause he couldn't talk with the asthma and all. Wearing the respirator.

Thanks, Marina—I should just get a tattoo that says that. *Thanks, Marina.* Because if like you're going to be trapped on a mountain for the firepocalypse, you want to be with the beautiful firefighter, right?

The beautiful, brilliant, *innovative* firefighter! You said it, Robert, not me! How did we get so lucky? Work with what you got, right?

Can you hand me that flashlight, please?

Isn't this amazing? Hermanos, this is just such a fucking amazing thing, I can't even say it. Every wall, he covered every wall. The one thing all this charcoal is good for—you can draw with it! I never even knew that.

Isn't it amazing? This is like, you see those cave paintings and you think, how did this last for a hundred thousand years? Or however many years—ten thousand, I dunno. Maybe some guy painted them when no one was looking during the World Cup. I never actually saw one, just pictures and that 3D movie. Point is, it lasted all that time.

So Hermanos is a magician—an illusionist, yeah—and I hope maybe you can figure out a way to do some of that shit for us. Maybe disappear us from here back home. That would be nice.

But the fact is, he's an artist, too, and he drew all this, and I just think it's fucking amazing. Like someday in ten thousand years, someone will find this bunker and see it and they'll understand what happened. A picture story without words. Maybe Jeff's batteries will last ten thousand years and they can watch it on his phone. Cause there sure as shit ain't gonna be anything left out there to show them what happened.

Yeah okay, okay, I'm sorry, *lo siento*. I should get a tattoo with that, too, right? *I'm sorry* in every language. Hermanos, could you do that? It would be cool if we could all get matching tattoos.

Look, I really *am* sorry. Really. Aw, Jeff, come on. Marina, I know. I said I'm sorry. Lula. I know we all feel the same way. We just show it different.

This is me. I'm sorry this is me. But that's why it's good we have everyone else.

Yeah, I'd like to stay down here too. It's definitely cooler. Not like we're missing much up there.

I did go up to the tower really early this morning, while it was still dark. No, I was with Marina, I didn't break any goddamn rules. Robert was there too. Not that I could understand what he was saying. Physics, that should be a language, too.

It *is* a language? Yeah? How do you say "I'm sorry" in physics?

Anyway, it was strange. In the day everything's all hazed out by the smoke. Looks like fucking Mordor out there. At night it does too, but you can see the fire better in the dark.

Can you even tell anymore if it's day or night? If this keeps up. I wonder about that sometimes. Anyway we're up there on the tower and it's night, it's dark, you can't see anything, *really* can't see anything because of the smoke, so no stars, I don't even know if you could ever see lights here from houses or something, because the whole three days I've been here it's just smoke.

Marina? Before, could you see lights?

So okay, some, but not now. Not this morning. No moon, *nada*, *oscura*, no nothing. Just dark.

Except for, up there on the tower, if you turned in a circle, you could see the fire, this ring of fire. Shut up, I hate that song. Jeff, serious, bra, shut up. A perfect ring of fire, *so perfect*—it was beautiful, I couldn't make this up. You could see it moving but it was like someone had designed it, like special effects. Like Marina says, fire is a living thing—that's what it was like. A living thing. Only so big, you can't imagine any living thing could be that big. Huge. *Enorme. Vasto.*

And it's here. It's right here. Right there.

No, I won't. I haven't finished yet. Let me finish.

Thanks.

This is the other thing, we were out there watching and eventually it got light. Sunrise only no sun, it just got light. Lighter. All you could see was smoke and you could definitely smell it more, I could smell it more—everyone did, I know. You couldn't see the fire so much but I assume it's there, right, Marina?

Look, there's no point, we can't fucking pretend! And it's my fucking turn. And the thing is, as it got light—lighter—Marina and Robert and me looked at the sky and we saw clouds. Big clouds, far away but dark, not those other clouds that are just the smoke and dust. Real clouds. And the wind, you all felt the wind, right? I know it's hot, we all get that, but it's wind. You could feel it now, if we were outside. Dr. Science there, he can tell you, wind means a front coming in. A front.

I don't know what kind of front. Santa Ana? I know it's the wrong time of year but now we get those crazy winds all the time. Yeah, see, Marina says the same thing, and that's like her *job*. But we don't know what kind. It could be, it could be it's just blowing towards us, all of it, and—

But it could be, maybe, maybe it's rain. Those kind of clouds, tell them what they are, Robert.

Mammatus, right. Mammatus clouds. Big thunderstorms, they can be part of a severe storm, with rain, maybe. Rain, real rain, a ton of rain . . .

Right? Right? Maybe? Yeah.

Can we go up back there to the fire tower, Marina? All of us? It'll be dark soon but if we go up now it'll be easier on the steps. Then everyone could see what I was talking about. The way it looks at night, the fire. I think everyone should see it, I think everyone might want to see it. So afterwards you can say you saw it, maybe. And if not, just so we can all see it together.

Yeah, we can have a vote. I don't think we should leave anyone behind—that's not for me to decide, we all need to—okay, that's cool, everyone says yes. Marina, you can do the honors? And Robert, you and me, we can go at the end, in case anyone needs—yeah, it's a long freaking way, you will definitely get winded, Lula. It's fine with me if you keep those things on, you and Hermanos. I know it's my turn but I'll wait cause I want you to see up there. And you need them more than I do. Especially now. Too bad we don't have spacesuits. Spacesuits to breathe. But thank god we have two respirators. Thank god for the U.S. Fire Service. Thank god for Marina.

Jeff, you got that one charger left, right? Now's the time, bra. Maybe. Roll 'em!

It does smell different up here, right? Right? I bet you can smell it even with those respirators on. The smoke but something else, I think maybe there's something else. Something not smoke.

Did you see that? Did anyone see that? Was it, do you think—lightning? Yeah? Maybe? Maybe.

Yeah, I know it could be a goddamn terrorist drone. But it also could be lightning. So it could, something could happen. Rain. It might happen is all I'm saying.

Anyway, we're all here. It's like a movie, here we all are, the fuck we would ever know each other but here we are. I wonder if anyone else . . .

Okay. Okay. That's it for me. Thanks—really, thank you. You don't know what it's like—but of course you do. I know you do. Even Jeff. So okay, I'm done. I'm done. So.

Everyone gather round. Everyone hold hands.

Whose turn is it?

Beyond Belief: On Becoming a Writer

I DECIDED TO BECOME a writer in the summer of 1962, when I was five years old. My mother took me to see *The Wonderful World of the Brothers Grimm*, a fantasia with George Pal Puppetoons and claymation dragons and the austerely beautiful, melancholy young Laurence Harvey as Wilhelm Grimm, neglecting his day job to collect folk tales and each night bringing them to life as he scribbles in his garret room. Near the end of the movie, Wilhelm lies in his garret close to death: he has forsaken his writing, and it's literally killing him.

And then they begin to come, climbing through the window and creeping from beneath his desk: giants and princesses, fairies and dragons and Red Riding Hood, all the creatures of his stories, all the magic that had been locked inside his head, loosed now and arriving to plead with him not to die. Without Wilhelm (they tell him) there will be no stories; without him they will all die and be forgotten. No Singing Bone; no elves; no wise women or dragons or brave boys named Jack.

And see now, the storyteller rallies: when next we glimpse Wilhelm he's bent over his desk, papers everywhere and his dull commissions forever forgotten. Cue theme music and leather-bound volume of Märchen; cue my five-year-old-self in the audience, crying and utterly transported by the vision of the man in the attic room surrounded by all he had given birth to: this was how I was going to spend my life!

First, however, I had to learn to read and write.

I was in many ways the eidos of the fledgling writer: bespectacled, often sick with asthma, lying in bed and reading *The Jungle Books*, *The Call of the Wild*, *The Wolf King*, *The Big Golden Book of Elves and Fairies*; good in school, part of a huge gang of children that each afternoon played Ringolevio and Hide and Seek in the idyllic little Yonkers cul-de-sac where we lived. Every weekend we would drive across the small city to where my paternal grandparents' house overlooked the Hudson, a great rambling old house with eight fireplaces and six bathrooms—six!—built around 1900 and filled with the strange things my lawyer grandfather had bought at auction during the Depression: tapestries, swords, Roman coins and daggers, oriental rugs everywhere underfoot, a Hudson River School painting that had been repaired where one of my cousins shot an arrow through it. And clocks, scores and scores of clocks, from pocket watches with little silver skulls for fobs to the huge grandfather clock that stood in the foyer, a clock big enough to hide in, though no one ever did. There was an ornate little porcelain holy water stoup by the front entry, nearly as marvelous as all those bathrooms; in the winding stairway to the third floor, the stuffed head of a caribou that my father had shot when he was sixteen. In the attic room, once a nursery, there were all the books my father and aunts and uncles had once read, along with strange, slightly sad relics of ancient holidays: Halloween noisemakers, pasteboard Santas with dirty white wool beards and gilt gowns; an enormous box full of toy guns that my brothers and boy cousins would raid immediately upon our arrival.

From the attic I could look down the broad slow black girth of the Hudson and see the lights of the George Washington Bridge; directly across the river were the brilliant arabesques of the roller coaster at Palisades Amusement Park, where there would be fireworks in the summer, and the words PALISADES AMUSEMENT PARK floating above the cliffs like a banner from a dream. On the veranda outside his study my grandfather had set up a telescope, so that I could observe the ominous miracle of the sun going down behind the Palisades, a crimson disk at once beautiful and terrifying, bitten away by the cliffs and the skeleton of a roller coaster.

This is the house I called Lazyland (a name that did come in a dream) in my novel *Glimmering*, and Fairview in *Illyria*; this is the house behind so many of my books, a world within the world, wonderful and faintly terrifying, where the last sound I heard at night was my grandfather's footsteps as he paced slowly from floor to floor, stopping all the clocks so that their concerted chiming would not wake his dreaming grandchildren.

When I was eight, our favorite babysitter gave me two paperback books. One was John Steinbeck's *The Red Pony*; the other something called *The Hobbit*. I loved animals and animal stories, and had expanded my career plans slightly to include becoming a zoologist. But I didn't like horses, and so *The Red*

Pony remains unread. *The Hobbit*, however, looked strange, and there was a slight whiff of the Alpine in its cover image of mountains: I was suspicious that it might be something like *Heidi*. Still, its very oddity seduced me—the title made no sense—and so one day I began to read it. That was when my life changed again, an experience intensified when I read *The Lord of the Rings* a year later and, immediately upon completing it, turned to page one and read it all over again.

This of course has been the Ur Experience of so many of us who became fantasy writers after 1960 or so; but back then, for me at least, this was a journey into literary Terra Incognita. There was yet no fantasy publishing industry; there were no signposts showing me to other books like these (a helpful brochure from the Westchester County Library Commission suggested that readers who enjoyed *The Hobbit* might also like George Orwell's *Animal Farm*).

And so I simply read Tolkien over and over and over again, until Lin Carter's *A Look Behind "The Lord of the Rings"* appeared in 1969. By then we had moved from Yonkers to a small, semi-rural town sixty miles north of Manhattan. I became the ugly, smart New Girl at St Patrick's School, and Tolkien's world became even more a haven for me, until another smart new girl arrived—Janine, who, miraculously, had also read Tolkien!—and my social life became more pleasant. After school I wandered in the woods for hours, pretending I was an Abenaki Indian and making snares to catch rabbits (I never did).

But at night I pored over Lin Carter's book, which provided a map of sorts to the world Beyond The Fields We

Know: the inspiration for Tolkien's work in the *Elder Eddas* and Icelandic sagas, Middle English lays and *Beowulf*; the work of other writers like C.S. Lewis and Lord Dunsany, E.R. Eddison, and Charles Williams. I began to track down all of these. The town librarian ordered me a copy of *Beowulf*, its pages alternating between modern and old English, and I read this painstakingly; she also found me a volume of the Norse Myths, and the *Eddas*, and (with some shaking of her head amid warnings that I wouldn't like it, which I didn't) Edmund Spenser's *The Faerie Queene*.

And then Lin Carter himself began editing the Adult Fantasy Series at Ballantine, Tolkien's American paperback publishers, and I would order each title as it became available: *The Worm Ouroboros*; *The Well at the World's End*; *Lud-in-the-Mist*; *Dragons, Elves, and Heroes*; *The Island of the Mighty*; *Red Moon and Black Mountain*. The library had all of Lord Dunsany, oddly enough, with the original Sid Simes illustrations (my favorite was captioned "There the Gibbelins lived and discreditably fed"), and for my thirteenth birthday my mother gave me the only thing I wanted, Jorge Luis Borges's just-published-in-English *The Book of Imaginary Beings*.

I was writing my own stories by this time. Ghost stories ("The Soul of Caliban"), versions of the Greek myths I loved, epic fantasy novels—*The Unicorn's Amulet*, *The Dragon-Harp of Faerie*, *The Quest for the Black Unicorn*. I've never gone back to read these, but I vividly recall how dark they were. My protagonists had a knack for going slowly, irrecoverably mad, and the landscapes they gazed upon were wastelands, populated by gods and beings that brought only pain or, at best, a terrible yearning that could never be assuaged. Parn, the hero of one book, looks out his castle window one night and has a vision of the blind god Othiym, a beautiful, terrible Dionysian figure who rides a stag that bellows in pain at the god's touch. The vision drives Parn to leave home in search of the malign god; he never finds Othiym (I never finished the story) but I used the name years later for the maleficent lunar goddess of *Waking the Moon.*

These were the taproots of my story tree. Thinking back, I'm struck by how little I've strayed from them, and also by what a long time it took for me to learn to actually write a story. I was an arrogant and confident adolescent, too arrogant even to take touch-typing lessons in high school, something I've always regretted. As a teenager I became stagestruck, going to Broadway as often as I could and each summer going with my mother to see all the plays in rep at the American Shakespeare Theater in nearby Stratford, Connecticut. I joined a local theatre group and wrote plays for them, an adaptation of Lewis Carroll's Alice books (I played Alice; she went mad) and, with my friend Janine, a number of fractured fairy tales, including "Tales of the Bedragoned Buffoon" and "The Silly Situation at the Ravastan School," featuring a proto-Hogwarts castle, where youngsters apply themselves to The Study of Advanced Folly, and a villainous sorcerer named The Wart of Peckindorf. When the time came to go to college I decided on Catholic University in Washington, DC, a city I'd fallen in love with on my eighth-grade class trip.

CU had a famed acting program and a gorgeous new theatre complex that housed the Drama Department. I joined the intensive Bachelor of Fine Arts program, majoring in play-writing but with my career plans once again revamped—they now included acting and directing. Noel Coward was my role model. But within the first few weeks I bombed. I had a disastrous freshman audition, one of those make-or-break scenarios before the entire Drama Department faculty and graduate and postgraduate student body. The careers of undergraduate actors were determined by this audition. I bombed spectacularly, doing a pastiche of the fool Feste's speeches from *Twelfth Night*, but had the presence of mind to remain on the stage afterward and announce that I was available for tech work. So I was busy, at least, doing assistant stage manager work and running lights and sound in the Callen Theatre, and doing prop work on the Hartke Main Stage.

I got a job as an usher for the American debut of two short Tom Stoppard plays, *Dirty Linen* and *New-Found-Land*, and every night watched Stoppard himself at the back of the theatre, observing the performance. The play's kindly director knew I was an aspiring playwright and urged me to talk to Stoppard, but I was far too shy; though one night Stoppard spoke to me, taking my hand and turning it over curiously, then pronouncing, "You do have black fingernails!" I was writing, too, absurdist one-acts equally inspired by Ionesco and Woody Allen. I had started a new book, something called *The Amleth Union*, about a group of friends discovering the existence of an ancient, supernatural order on the grounds of their university in Washington, DC.

Mostly, however, I ran wild, exploring the city with my beloved friend O.J., drinking heavily, taking drugs, having indiscriminate sex, getting involved in the nascent punk scene between New York and DC. I had a few years earlier taken to heart Rimbaud's *Lettre Voyante*: To be a poet, one must become a seer. One becomes a seer through a deliberate derangement of all the senses. I told myself I would do this until I was thirty, and then settle down to a serious life as a writer. My academic career took a nosedive as dramatic as my audition. I went from being the only freshman on the Dean's List, with a 4.0 average, to flunking out, in just three years. My friends had all gotten their acts together; they were completing their degrees and going on to jobs and lives and relationships (all save O.J., who was exhibiting the first signs of what became a terrible and tragic mental illness). I felt like Falstaff abandoned by Prince Hal. In disgrace, I went home to live with my parents, and—the final ignominy—took a low-paying job at a bookstore.

Somehow, throughout all of this, I wrote. In my freshman year I shared first prize in the university's C.W. Stoddard Fiction Award, for a dark short story called "Lords," in which a Dionysian god preys upon the children of Kamensic Village, a fictionalized version of my hometown. The prize consisted of fifty bucks and a case of Heineken, which I drank in triumph with my friends on the roof of the building that housed the campus literary magazine. I also inherited the mantle of the magazine's editor, a responsibility I absolved myself of after a year (not fast enough). I dabbled at the libretto for a Brechtian musical version of *Beowulf*; several terrible, brittle comedies in the Coward mode; some short absurdist plays. The Theatre of the Absurd was made for me: nothing had to make any sense. Nothing needed to have a proper ending, or even a proper beginning. I also ran a thriving black market business, writing term papers for other students. I charged a dollar a page, plus a six-pack of beer and a carton of cigarettes; and would settle in front of my old Royal Upright typewriter, chain-smoking and drinking as I wrote about *Frankenstein* or *King Lear* or *Dune*—there was a popular course on science fiction and fantasy being offered by the English Department, and I thought it incredible that students couldn't be bothered to read *Dune*.

I got As in my playwriting class, and in anthropology, but nothing else. I seldom showed up for classes, and every Sunday night offered the same dilemma: to catch up with my studies, or catch the bus down to the Biograph Theater in Georgetown with O.J. and take in a double bill of Truffaut or Fellini or Buñuel? Week after week I'd ask myself, "Twenty years from now, what will matter: that you did well on this test or that you saw *Amarcord*?" Week after week I'd make the same decision. I saw the Ramones' first DC gig; Talking Heads playing a pre-Christmas show for an audience of about ten people (one of them was David Byrne's mother, who invited me for dinner at their house in Baltimore); numerous small club performances by Patti Smith; an unforgettable Springsteen show in the Georgetown University gymnasium.

But at some point during my brief tenure in the Drama Department, I burned out on theatre. There were only so many times I could read *Oedipus Rex*, only so many times I could watch university productions of *Macbeth* and *A Man for All Seasons*, even with Paul Scofield in the wings, hitting up on my classmates. The more plays I read (and performed in—despite my failed audition, I acted in small student productions and scenes, playing the ghost in *Blithe Spirit* and Mrs X. in Strindberg's *The Other*, among others), the more I realized that there is a very small, finite number of great plays, and I was not ever going to write one of them.

The realization chastened me, but it was also a relief. Great plays are collaborative efforts between author, director, actor, designer; a play's ultimate glory is not upon the printed page but the proscenium. I was too much of a loner, and too arrogant, to be good at this collaborative process. Plus, I used too many words; a liability in playwriting.

But I loved the feeling of power that came from creating contemporary characters, people I might see on the street, and moving them around on the page; though this was offset by a sense of constriction, that I couldn't make use of the more visionary, supernatural effects I liked to play with in my stories. I had for some time been working at a science fiction novel, much influenced by the work of Angela Carter, and Samuel R. Delany's *Dhalgren*, a story set in a far-future Washington, DC, where the trees and vegetation had run amok, and a guild of prostitutes lived in the ruins of Embassy Row. I didn't get very far on my story—I always did much more thinking about writing than I did actual writing—but the image of the city I loved overgrown with roses and decay remained in my head for years, until it finally became the poisonous bloom of *Winterlong*.

Yet I still didn't know how to write, except in the roughest, most intuitive fashion. Convinced of my innate talent, I refused to take any writing classes (save playwriting, which was required). I had a rude awakening when a story I submitted to *The New Yorker* was rejected, though with a very kind note from an editor, who noted my obvious debts to Richard Brautigan and Frederick Exley and gently suggested I concentrate on plotting—advice which I have to this day pretty much ignored. Plot remains a distant fourth for me, behind character and setting and the evocation of pure emotional experience.

Since high school days, I had kept notebooks in which I wrote about people I knew. I would hitchhike to Katonah, the real-life model for my fictionalized Kamensic Village, and sit there and observe kids my own age, teenagers I knew only slightly or not at all, and record their actions and conversations. I did the same in college, writing about my friends. This caused problems when a girlfriend read my notebook without my knowledge; she was appalled by the detached, clinical descriptions of herself and our circle, and I couldn't say much in my own defense (except for warning her not to read somebody else's journal without permission). I've never been good at Making Things Up; nearly all of the characters in my fiction are based upon real people, and there is a certain vampiric guilt in this process of observation and distillation, though the final characterization is nearly always pretty remote from its original inspiration. It was as a teenager that I also developed the habit of fixating on individuals as erotic and creative muses, people who, sometimes for years or even decades, have served as prisms for my work. Often these aren't people I know well (though sometimes they are), and nearly always there is a physical or chronological distance between myself and the person I'm writing about.

One thing I did take from my years of studying acting is the habit of observation, of trying to fit into another's skin so acutely that one can mimic the other's moves, the tenor of his or her breathing. I am very conscious when writing or attempting to find the right cast for my work, drawing on people I know in the process; and very often when a character doesn't work it's not a matter of plot dynamics so much as miscasting—A should be played by a drag king, not a male-to-female transsexual; B should be a dying astronaut rather than a patrician WASP woman.

These revelations often come to me in dreams. "Snow on Sugar Mountain" only came to life after I dreamed of an elderly man, an astronaut dying of cancer, who was struggling to climb the rusted scaffolding of one of the missile towers at the Redstone Arsenal, reaching futilely for the full moon in the sky above him when he at last reached the top. Up until then, the story's central character was a dying woman I had lived with and cared for, over the course of several weeks when I was nineteen. I began the story not long after she died, but it was some years before the dream came to me and the story finally came together.

Still, dreaming wasn't going to help me much while I was working at a bookstore. I did reconnect with my old drama group and write another play for them, *The Misadventures of MaryAnna Maudlin and the Dreadful Things That Befell Her* but I had an overwhelming sense of being exiled from The Land of Eternal Youth to The Land of the Underemployed. My boyfriend, W., was in DC and many of my friends were now living in Manhattan, so I spent as much time as possible on various trains, shuttling between my parents' house and the two cities. It was during one of these trips, on March

17, a few weeks before my twenty-second birthday, that I was abducted and raped while visiting W. in Washington. Until then I had always envisioned myself as the heroine of my own life, triumphing over adversity—even the bookstore became a Dickensian backdrop to the story I was always telling myself about myself: a New York fixture, it had been around for decades and was run by three generations of the same family. Suddenly my storyline changed.

I had been raised Catholic, but the concept of evil was, in those post–Vatican II days, very much a relative thing, at least as it was taught to me in the Catholic schools I attended, and all the dark gods and godlings I wrote about in my stories were pretty much window-dressing. When I was raped, I saw for the first time that evil was real, and impartial, and utterly random. It was a terrifying realization, and the vision I had then never left me: that if you peeled back the surface of this world, you would see the real world beneath, the world that was, is, a wasteland. It's the vision that most of my fictional protagonists have at some point, and one that I now have to fight in my waking life.

At the time, though, I was determined to act as though nothing happened. In retrospect this seems ridiculous: when I first saw the opening of David Lynch's *Twin Peaks*, with its vision of a battered girl coming across a railroad trestle, I recognized myself, running screaming down the middle of a street near the DC riot corridor. I had thought I was going to be murdered; how could I ever have pretended it didn't matter? But in the aftermath I did what I had always done, what I always do: attempt to transmute my own experience into a story, with a coherent narrative and a resolution that, even if it's not a happy one, offers some closure to the reader. And there was more Bad Stuff to be endured: the emergency room doctor who treated me after the rape told me that he detected some sort of growth inside me, and advised me to see a doctor immediately. But I was in shock, and completely forgot his warning until I was home some days later and was examined by my mother's gynecologist, who then sent me to another specialist, who called in his partners, who eventually all confirmed that I had a large tumor on my ovary. In those pre-sonogram days, there was no way of determining if this might be benign, or ovarian cancer; the doctors were pragmatic, telling me they weren't certain what they would find when they went inside: the growth was large, and if it was cancerous there was not a lot they would be able to do to treat it. Surgery was scheduled for the first available slot, which wasn't for several weeks. I didn't have health insurance, but the surgeon agreed to let me pay over time.

I continued to work at the bookstore, earning my $97.00 a week. At night I helped rehearse *MaryAnna Maudlin*. As it turned out, I missed the performances: I was in the hospital. I underwent surgery, feeling as though I'd never left the nightmarish emergency room at DC General; one ovary and fallopian tube had been devoured by tumors, which were removed. At one point during recovery I half-woke and sat up, dazed: I saw my father in a chair watching me, his face anguished: the results of the biopsy had not come back yet. I looked at him and almost immediately passed out again. When hours later I finally woke again, the surgeon was there, beaming as he held up the results of the biopsy: benign. I spent the next few days in the hospital recovering and reading John Fowles' *The Magus* while shot full of Demerol. Two days after being released, I quit my job at the bookstore and moved back to DC to live with W.

This was May, 1979. That summer, W. and I and a group of friends squatted in a house in Turkey Thicket with no electricity or plumbing; from the front window, I could see the abandoned gas station where I'd been abducted in March. I got a job at the Smithsonian's National Air and Space Museum—I had worked there the previous summer—and by the end of the summer we'd moved to a small apartment complex nearby, where several dozen of our friends already lived.

For the next six years I had a rather idyllic, punky *Friends*-style existence, working at NASM by day and spending a lot of time at clubs at night. I got readmitted to the university and entered the Anthropology Department, paying the exorbitant tuition costs myself and getting straight As this time. I was still working a full-time job and carrying a heavy party schedule. Cocaine and speed helped immeasurably in all this, but when after two years I finally got my degree I quit all drugs cold turkey, as I'd quit chain smoking a few years before.

W., an English major who had a wonderful gift as an editor, encouraged my writing and gave me a self-correcting electric typewriter, a godsend for someone who couldn't type and who rewrote obsessively. During the week I'd get up at 4 or 5 a.m. and write for several hours before going off to NASM; on weekend nights I'd sit at the typewriter with a drink at my elbow (and the occasional cigarette) and write with the stereo blasting. I was working on a supernatural novel set in Texas, where my mother grew up and where I'd spent my summers as a girl. Texas in those days had some of the same appeal that Maine did when I first moved here fifteen years ago, a sense of a place mired in time—the Texas of my childhood and adolescence was still in many ways the Texas my mother had known—and I loved losing myself there.

W., who worked as a bartender and thus had a schedule opposite mine, would read my story and line-edit it, and I would painstakingly rewrite it, repeating the process sometimes a dozen times before a story or chapter would improve. I was, without being conscious of it, already deep into the pattern that much of my later writing would take: using my own experience, using people I knew, and casting a supernatural haze over the mostly realistic setting. And through W. I met one of the most important people in my life, my friend and sometime collaborator Paul Witcover, W.'s cousin. We met the night before Paul left to attend the Clarion Writers' Workshop, at a dinner organized by Paul's mother. For some time she'd been it trying to get the two of us together—we liked the same music, she said, we liked the same writers—but I was deeply suspicious of the prospect.

Wrong again. Paul and I met and it was like two of those little magnetic Scotty Dogs clicking: we loved the same music! We loved the same books! For the first time in my life I had a conversation with someone who knew Patti Smith AND *Triton* AND Philip K. Dick AND Iggy Pop. The next morning Paul left for Clarion and I was consumed with envy when at the end of the summer he returned, having already sold his first story. But he read my stories and critiqued them and offered more encouragement; and when Paul sold another story I slowly, slowly began to see that this might really be possible, that in spite of everything I might be able to get published too.

But not yet. I had one completed story, called "King Heroin," that I bounced around to *F&SF* and various men's magazines where I knew Stephen King had published early in his career. My favorite rejection letter of this time came from an editor who wrote "I really, really enjoyed your story, but right now we are looking for more Sex-Oriented Material." (I kept the rejection letters in the freezer; I can't recall why.) W. worshipped John Gardner, so I bought and read Gardner's *On Becoming a Novelist*, and was exhilarated to learn that, according to Gardner, I had a writer's nature and a writer's instincts, even if mine were crude and undeveloped. The knack for entering what Gardner calls "the vivid and continuous dream" of fiction; an eye for seeing strangeness in everyday life; the belief in the supremacy of character over plot: I knew this stuff, even if I was still learning (am still learning) how to communicate it.

"Strangeness is the one quality in fiction that cannot be faked," Gardner wrote: when I read those words I had the same sense I did when I met Paul: that I had, at last, come home.

It was around this time, the early 1980s, that a miracle occurred. NASM became one of the first places in the country to get word processors for all its employees. I spent two weeks being trained with other NASM employees, and returned to my cubicle to find my own computer. I literally got goosebumps: I knew my life had changed. No more retyping; no more time wasted on revisions that would now take minutes rather than hours or days. I began staying after work and writing. I abandoned my Texas novel and revisions of "King Heroin" and instead started or revived several projects—what W. derisively called my mutant prostitute story; something called *Eighth Moon*, about a woman anthropologist finding remnants of an ancient goddess cult; my university story *The Amleth Union*. One day during my lunch hour I walked to a shop called The Artifactory and spent a huge chunk of my paycheck on a beautiful Balinese puppet. When I returned to work I set it on my desk, announced to my friend Greg that "This is going to bring me luck," and began working on a story called "Prince of Flowers" (on company time, too: your U.S. tax dollars at work!).

I broke up with W., though for several years he continued to edit me, and moved to Capitol Hill. I met N., who became one of the muses for *Waking the Moon*. I quit my job at NASM and briefly took a high-paying job for a UK defense contractor. I started spending weekends in Charlottesville, Virginia, where N.'s best friend, Eddie Dean (now a journalist) drove an ice cream truck into the strange, archaic countryside of the surrounding Green Mountains, another place where time seemed to have stopped. N. agreed to help support me so I could write, so I quit my job and started doing temp work, taking jobs for a month at a time, then taking a month off to write. "On the Town Route" came out of this period, and "Engels Unaware," "Snow on Sugar Mountain," and "The Boy in the Tree," the novella that became *Winterlong*. I wrote feverishly, knowing I had only a short time to finish a story. I collected more rejection slips, my favorite from the editor of *Weird Tales*, who told me that "Snow on Sugar Mountain" was too bizarre for him.

Ah! I thought. I've written something too weird for *Weird Tales*! But I consoled myself with John Gardner's words: "Strangeness is the one quality in fiction that cannot he faked." I had during these months the burgeoning sense that I was, at last, being born; that I was going to break through.

But not yet.

In 1986 I took my first writing workshop, taught by Richard Grant at the Writer's Center in Bethesda. I was still doing temp work, and for a while worked a second job at Second Story Books in Bethesda, another oddly Dickensian experience (I toyed with the idea of writing a play about this, called *Shelf Life*). Richard was the first published novelist I had ever met, and it was several weeks before I submitted my first story, a revision of "Prince of Flowers." When I received back the copy of my manuscript, annotated with Richard's distinctive penmanship and peacock-blue ink, I almost wept.

"A lovely story, almost a tour-de-force of linguistic and sensual prose . . ." It was the first time a published writer, other than my friend Paul, had read something I wrote.

I had not yet sent out "Prince of Flowers," but now I did—to Tappan King at *Twilight Zone Magazine*, which was a powerhouse in those boom days for horror. After almost a year, the story was rejected. I was devastated. I was also furious, because I knew the story had never been seen by an editor, and I was convinced that I had finally written something worth publishing. Not a great story—I knew that—but absolutely a *Twilight Zone* story.

And this is when someone suddenly really did become the hero of my life: Paul Witcover, who was now reading slush for *Twilight Zone*. I sent him "Prince of Flowers"; and Paul passed it on to Tappan. Within a few weeks the letter arrived that I had been waiting for almost my whole life, saying that "Prince of Flowers" had been accepted. It was published in the February 1987 issue, first in the series of "Twilight Zone Firsts" featuring newly discovered writers.

After that, the other stories that I had already written began to find homes, slowly but steadily. And slowly but steadily I began to turn fragments of dreams I'd had into novels: *Winterlong*, the first chapters of *Waking the Moon*. The wasteland remained, in my life as in my fiction; but I had finally found a way to walk through it to the other side.

The night before I had my surgery, I had a dream. In the hospital I was calm but terrified, convinced that I had ovarian cancer; that the disastrous turning my life had taken on that March night just six weeks before meant that this was the way the story was going to turn out. In the dream I was walking beneath a midnight sky to where a long, rectangular marble pool stretched before me. The pool was like something from ancient Greece: white marble, black water; absolutely still. A number of objects floated upon its surface. As I drew to the pool's edge I saw that these were hyacinth blossoms, white and luminous, inutterably strange and beautiful. I knelt to look at them. That was when I saw that each blossom had been severed from its stalk. They were all dead.

Grief and horror overwhelmed me. I began to cry, then reached for one of the blossoms, drawing it toward me.

And realized that I was wrong. Because while I could clearly see where the flower had been hacked from its stem, it was not dead. The wound had closed up, and not just with this blossom, but all of them. I gazed out at the pool, black water, white hyacinths; and with amazement saw that they were all still blooming, every single one; beautiful and, miraculously, alive.

Coda: It's been more than a dozen years since I wrote this essay. During that time I've published seven more books and two more collections of short fiction, along with numerous book reviews, articles, and essays. My fiction branched out into noir, with *Generation Loss* and its sequels, *Available Dark*, and *Hard Light*, novels that don't inhabit the realm of the fantastic but occasionally wander within sight of it. I officiated at the wedding of my dear friends Paul Witcover and the playwright Cynthia Babak. I continue to teach at various writing workshops, and six years ago joined the faculty of the Stonecoast MFA program in creative writing, where I've had the privilege of teaching and mentoring dozens of remarkable writers. I wrote *Illyria*, the one story I had been trying to write since I was seventeen. In my work I continue to explore the strange, beautiful, often terrifying worlds of numerous artists, real and fictional. Despite living in a real world that increasingly resembles that of one of my early dystopian novels, I consider myself a very lucky person.

Kronia

"Nothing sorts out memories from ordinary
moments. It is only later that they claim
remembrance, when they show their scars."
—Chris Marker, *La Jetée*

We never meet. Not never, fleetingly: five times in the last eighteen years. The first time I don't recall; you say it was late spring, a hotel bar. But I see you entering a restaurant five years later, stooping beneath the lintel behind our friend Andrew. You don't remember that.

We grew up a mile apart. The road began in Connecticut and ended in New York. A dirt road when we moved in, we both remember that; it wasn't paved till much later. We rode our bikes back and forth. We passed each other fifty-seven times. We never noticed. I fell once, rounding that curve by the golf course, a long scar on my leg now from ankle to knee, a crescent colored like a peony. Grit and sand got beneath my skin, there was blood on the bicycle chain. A boy with glasses stopped his bike and asked was I okay. I said yes, even though

I wasn't. You rode off. I walked home, most of the mile, my leg black, sticky with dirt, pollen, deerflies. I never saw the boy on the bike again.

We went to different schools. But in high school we were at the same party. Your end, Connecticut. How did I get there? I have no clue. I knew no one. A sad fat girl's house, a girl with red kneesocks, beanbag chairs. She had one album: The Shaggs. More sad girls, a song called "Foot Foot." You stood by a table and ate pretzels and drank so much Hi-C you threw up. I left with my friends. We got stoned in the car and drove off. A tall boy was puking in the azaleas out front.

Wonder what he had? I said.

Another day. The New Canaan Bookstore, your end again. I was looking at a paperback book.

That's a good book, said a guy behind me. My age, sixteen or seventeen. Very tall, springy black hair, wire-rimmed glasses. You like his stuff?

I shook my head. No, I said. I haven't read it. I put the book back. He took it off the shelf again. As I walked off I heard him say *Time Out of Joint.*

We went to college in the same city. The Metro hadn't opened yet. I was in Northeast, you were in Northwest. Twice we were on the same bus going into Georgetown. Once we were at a party where a guy threw a drink in my face.

Hey! yelled my boyfriend. He dumped his beer on the guy's head.

You were by the table again, watching. I looked over and saw you laugh. I started laughing too, but you immediately looked down then turned then walked away.

Around that time I first had this dream. I lived in the future. My job was to travel through time, hunting down evildoers. I kept running into the same man, my age, darkhaired, tall. Each time I saw him my heart lurched. We kissed furtively, beneath a table while bullets zipped overhead, beside a waterfall in Hungary. For two weeks we hid in a shack in the Northwest Territory, our radio dying, waiting to hear that the first wave of fallout had subsided. A thousand years, back and forth, the world reshuffled. Our child was born, died, grew old, walked for the first time. Sometimes your hair was grey, sometimes black. Once your glasses shattered when a rock struck them. You still have the scar on your cheek. Once I had an abortion. Once the baby died. Once you did. That was just a dream.

You graduated and went to the Sorbonne for a year to study economics. I have never been to France. I got a job at NASA collating photographs of spacecraft. You came back and started working for the newspaper. Those years, I went to the movies almost every night. Flee the sweltering heat, sit in the Biograph's crippling seats for six hours, Pasolini, Fellini, Truffaut, Herzog, Weir. *La Jetée*, a lightning bolt: an illuminated moment when a woman's black-and-white face moves in the darkness. A tall man sat in front of me and I moved to another seat so I could see better; he turned and I glimpsed your face. Unrecognized: I never knew you. Later in the theater's long corridor you hurried past me, my head bent over an elfin spoonful of coke.

Other theaters. We didn't meet again when we sat through *Berlin Alexanderplatz*, though I did read your review. *Our*

Hitler was seven hours long; you stayed awake, I fell asleep halfway through the last reel, curled on the floor, but after twenty minutes my boyfriend shook me so I wouldn't miss the end.

How could I have missed you then? The theater was practically empty.

I moved far away. You stayed. Before I left the city I met your colleague Andrew: we corresponded. I wrote occasionally for your paper. You answered the phone sometimes when I called there.

You say you never did.

But I remember your voice: you sounded younger than you were, ironic, world-weary. A few times you assigned me stories. We spoke on the phone. I knew your name.

At some point we met. I don't remember. Lunch, maybe, with Andrew when I visited the city? A conference?

You married and moved three thousand miles away. E-mail was invented. We began to write. You sent me books.

We met at a conference: we both remember that. You stood in a hallway filled with light, midday sun fogging the windows. You shaded your eyes with your hand, your head slightly downturned, your eyes glancing upward, your glasses black against white skin. Dark eyes, dark hair, tall and thin and slightly stooped. You were smiling; not at me, at someone talking about the mutability of time. Abruptly the sky darkened, the long rows of windows turned to mirrors. I stood in the hallway and you were everywhere, everywhere.

You never married. I sent you books.

I had children. I never wrote you back.

You traveled everywhere: Paris, Beirut, London, Cairo, Tangier, Cornwall, Fiji. You sent me postcards. I never left this country.

I was living in London with my husband and children when the towers fell. I e-mailed you. You wrote back:

Oh sure, it takes a terrorist attack to hear from you!

I was here alone on the mountain when I found out. A brilliant cloudless day, the loons calling outside my window. I have no TV; I was online when a friend e-mailed me:

Terrorism. An airplane flew into the
World Trade Center. Bombs. Disaster

I tried to call my partner but the phone lines went down. I drove past the farmstand where I buy tomatoes and basil and stopped to see if anyone knew what had happened. A van was there with DC plates: the woman inside was talking on a cell phone and weeping. Her brother worked in one of the towers: he had rung her to say he was safe. The second tower fell. He had just rung back to say he was still alive.

When the phone lines were restored that night I wrote you. You didn't write back. I never heard from you again.

I was in New York. I had gone to Battery Park. I had never been there before. The sun was shining. You never heard from me again.

I had no children. At the National Zoo, I saw a tall man walking hand in hand with a little girl. She turned to stare at me: grey eyes, glasses, wispy dark hair. She looked like me.

Two years ago you came to see me here on the lake. We drank two bottles of champagne. We stayed up all night talking. You slept on the couch. When I said goodnight, I touched your forehead. I had never touched you before. You flinched.

Once in 1985 we sat beside each other on the Number 80 bus from North Capitol Street. Neither of us remembers that.

I was fifteen years old, riding my bike on that long slow curve by the golf course. The Petro Oil truck went by, too fast, and I lost my balance and went careening into the stone wall. I fell and blacked out. When I opened my eyes a tall boy with glasses knelt beside me, so still he was like a black-and-white photograph. A sudden flicker: for the first time he moved. He blinked, dark eyes, dark hair. It took a moment for me to understand he was talking to me.

"Are you okay?" He pointed to my leg. "You're bleeding. I live just down there—"

He pointed to the Connecticut end of the road.

He hid my ruined bike in the ferns. "Come on."

You put your arm around me and we walked very slowly to your house. A plane flew by overhead. This is how we met.

"Flying Squirrels in the Rafters"

Elizabeth Hand interviewed by Terry Bisson

You teach writing in New England. Anywhere else?

I'm on faculty at the Stonecoast MFA program here in Maine, but I also teach at various workshops across the country and have done so for about twenty-two years—Clarion and Clarion West, Odyssey, the Pike's Peak Writer's Conference, various other smaller workshops. I've also done workshops for elementary, high school, and college students—I especially love working with younger kids. A few years ago I did a series of poetry mini-workshops based on Arthur Rimbaud's life and work, with middle schoolers. It was a blast. This past summer I taught at Yale, which was fun but no different from any other writer's workshop, except for the setting, which was impressive.

When you teach writing, what do you try to unteach?

The habit of wanting to be a writer without first being a serious reader. I'm always taken aback by how many intelligent people set out to "be writers" (as opposed to simply writing) and have a very narrow repertoire of work they've actually read.

It's wonderful that so many people love Stephen King and Neil Gaiman—I do, too—but King and Gaiman are both well-read and widely read. That's one reason for their success. Watching movie and TV adaptations of books doesn't count.

I'm also continually surprised that many people just don't get how hard writing is to do. There are prodigies, as there are with any art, but for the rest of us there's a long, slow learning curve. Very few of us believe that we could sit down at the piano without having taken a course of study and bang out a challenging piano piece by Beethoven or Debussy or anyone else. But everyone thinks they can write a novel. That doesn't mean you need to have an undergraduate or graduate degree in writing—I don't—but you do need to put time in, learning your craft.

You studied theater in your misspent youth. Have you tried playwriting since? (Your colleague Jim Kelly has, and so have I, with spectacularly indifferent success.)

No, but in the last few years I've thought a lot about trying to write a play. I was in a very intense and competitive BFA program for theater, and after three years I realized that it was a lot harder to write even a mediocre play than I had imagined. I'd written four or five one-act plays for a children's/YA theater group when I was a teenager and seen them produced, which was a great experience. Transitioning from that to being a serious playwright was tough. I just didn't have the chops for it, and I didn't want to do something and fail miserably for the rest of my life. With fiction, I felt like I could fail miserably (and did), but eventually I might improve enough to succeed.

But I still love theater. There are a handful of performances I've seen in my life that changed me forever—a high school production of *Twelfth Night* which I saw when I was seventeen (the inspiration for my short novel *Illyria*); the Broadway preview of Tony Kushner's *Angels in America* in the early 1990s (which inspired me to write *Glimmering*).

One of things I most enjoy about living part of the year in London is having the opportunity to see amazing theater. Jez Butterworth's *Jerusalem* with Mark Rylance, which I saw in London a few years ago, is still inspiring me.

So yeah, I'd love to try to do that, but I need a good idea. Plays are tough.

I think of you as a modern American Pre-Raphaelite. You seem to plant one foot in the past and to regard the present as provisional, like an experiment that is spinning a little out of control. That's not a question, but it begs comment.

I don't think of myself that way, maybe because I tend to think of Pre-Raphaleites as beautiful young women with long flowing auburn tresses and blank gazes. But it's actually a good suss, if you go back to the origins of the Pre-Raphaelite Brotherhood. They had a foot in two camps—the world of early Renaissance painting, and that of modern Victorian London in the mid to late nineteenth century. I love the PRB—my novel *Mortal Love* is set partly in that world—but much of their work is kind of musty in contemporary terms, and their attitudes toward women could be pretty exploitative. Yet at the time they were considered rebels. There's a moral here, though I'm not sure I want to know what it is.

Throughout my career (and my life), I've definitely felt that the world we live in is an experiment that's spinning out of control. I've been writing dystopian, post-apocalyptic, and apocalyptic fiction for almost thirty years, long before it became popular. My taste for reading and writing it has diminished radically as I've seen our own world surpass the darkest visions that I or anyone else could come up with.

Rock music seems to play a large role in your fiction. Ever been in a band?

No. I have no musical talent whatsoever, but I love music and musicians and performers in general. I'm the consummate fan. In another life, I would have been a groupie. I am a very good dancer, though.

Why Maine? Do you heat with wood?

I fell in love with Maine when my family vacationed here when I was a kid. We went camping, in those old Sears Roebuck canvas screen tents—five kids (I'm the oldest) and our parents—and then later we'd rent a house on a lake in the Long Lakes region. My father used to come up to Maine to hunt and fish when he was young, and his stories also informed my own experience. So for me, as for a lot of other people, Maine was always this magical place.

I visited it again as an adult in the early 1980s, when a college friend of mine got married there—she grew up in the area where I now live. A bunch of her friends came up for the wedding and I fell in love with Maine all over again, especially the Maine islands and the coast, which was not where my family vacationed. In 1988, when my then-partner and I were looking for a place to move to from DC, we flipped a coin and chose the Maine coast.

I've been here ever since. I knew nothing of backwoods living, so I had to learn, fast. A close friend of mine from those days, an artist, said that this was a good place to be poor, and for some years we were very, very poor. I came from a middle-class suburban background, with little experience of How The Other Half Lives, and it was a real adjustment and often very scary to be poor. But I learned to get by, with the help of neighbors and friends and *The Tightwad Gazette*. It gave me a much better understanding of how poverty undermines lives in this country and an appreciation of how fortunate I was in my own upbringing. Americans don't like to factor luck into their life stories—everyone wants to believe she pulled herself up by her own bootstraps. Which a lot of people do, but I also took advantage of programs designed to help those with limited resources—WIC, HEAP, and so on. I don't have to anymore, and I'm grateful for that, but it enrages me to see politicians (like our current governor) attacking poor people and cutting the safety nets that helped me and so many others through tough times.

I do heat with wood—I learned about wood during our first winter at Tooley Cottage. I don't use wood at the cottage anymore, but we do use it at the house. In a typical winter we'll burn about four cords. I love heating with wood—we have a great stove with an isinglass window, so you can watch the flames. During the winter, which is about half the year, everyone lives around the woodstove.

Why Camden Town? Do you write there or just catch your breath?

My partner is a UK citizen and lives there, so for the last twenty-odd years I've spent a lot of time in Camden Town—not a "town" in the American sense but a district of London. I love it—it's very urban, gritty, totally counterpoint to where I live in Maine. It's very noisy—it's become a big tourist area, so there's lots of street life, lots of music, buskers, and drunks (many, *many* drunks) in addition to the normal vehicular traffic. I *do* work there, but for serious writing, I use the British Library or the Wellcome Library, both of which are about a twenty-minute walk.

But Camden Town is my London home. So yes, it's where I catch my breath and get some relief from stacking wood back in Maine.

In your novels there is almost always another hidden reality that intrudes on this one in alarming and often terrible or even beautiful ways. Is this a literary device or a deal you made with the Devil?

I could tell you, Terry, but then I'd have to sacrifice you on a stone slab beneath a full moon.

It's a literary device. But I've always wanted to believe in the existence of that other, hidden reality. In my writing I try to make it real and to depict it in as realistic a fashion as possible. I did have one uncanny experience when I was about thirteen, which I wrote about in "Near Zennor." Other than that, it's all wish fulfillment.

Cass Neary has been compared with Stieg Larsson's Liz Salander. What's the deal with these Scandinavian novelists? Does this have anything to do with global warming? Do you read mysteries? Why not?

I read some—I don't get to read enough for pleasure because of having to read grad student manuscripts and books for review. I've never read any of the Stieg Larsson books, or seen the movies—I tend to shy away from work to which my own books have been compared, not out of ego but so I can avoid being influenced. But I do love Nordic noir—I like reading about cold, miserable places. I'm going back to Sweden in a few weeks and will have the chance to meet some of the writers I admire. I'm excited about that!

And I do think the popularity of Nordic noir has something to do with global warming. So does the boom in adventure tourism in places like Iceland, Greenland, Antarctica, Alaska, Siberia, etc. With climate change, we're losing a large part of our world, in so many ways. Apart from the environmental and economic catastrophe, I think the loss of winter is going to be psychologically disruptive on a huge scale, at least for those of us in the Northern Hemisphere.

One sentence on each please: Amy Winehouse, Alison Bechdel, Paul Park.

Amy Winehouse sounds like she was teleported to our century from Swinging London circa 1966, one of my favorite eras: I love her, especially the song "Back to Black."

When I moved to Maine in 1988, some local alternative newspaper carried Bechdel's *Dykes to Watch Out For*, and reading that comic every week got me through some very tough years.

I've always believed that Paul Park and I are actually the same person split in two, like in that Platonic allegory of how the different genders came to be; he's a brilliant writer, and in person he makes me laugh harder than almost anyone else ever has.

You spend a lot of time dressing Cass Neary. Ever play with paper dolls? Ever consider licensing a Cass paper doll book?

Ha! I am *totally* going to come up with a Cass Neary paper doll book with my next publisher! That's brilliant.

I was not a doll fan as a girl. I loved stuffed animals, the more obscure the better. I had a Steiff mole, fox, bat, and a toy skunk made of real fur. I'd make my own stuffed animals, too—a flying squirrel, a raccoon.

I have very dim memories of a paper doll set, probably given to me when I was sick with chicken pox or measles and therefore desperate to be entertained. I did love doll houses—I loved rearranging the furniture. In another life, I'd be an interior designer. I also loved toy farms, where you could move around all the little farm animals. And dinosaurs.

But back to paper dolls. I am a closet clothes horse—as in, I have some very nice designer clothes that rarely leave my closet. I've bought them on eBay and at vintage or consignment shops over the years but only get to wear them at conventions or public readings or the like. Cass gets to wear them sometimes, even though she's six inches taller than me. We do have the same shoe size, though, and I own many pairs of cowboy boots, some Tony Lamas, which I started buying when I was a teenager visiting my mother's family in Texas. I have ostrich boots, eelskin, lizard, and a really great pair of violet python boots. I hardly ever wear them—as Cass learned, Maine is a really bad place to wear cowboy boots, especially in the winter. The first time I was in Reykjavik I almost killed myself, wearing my Tony Lamas in bad weather.

My real-life everyday wardrobe is Cass's and has been for the past forty years. Boatneck shirts, black jeans, black cashmere sweaters, Converse sneakers, boots. I don't wear heels and never have. Nearly everything I own is secondhand. A lot of it has seen better days. Cass would understand.

You and Paul Witcover did a comic together, right? Do you keep up with the "industry" today? Do you read graphic novels?

I have to admit that I don't even try to keep up anymore—there's just too much stuff, and too much great stuff, out there.

That's not to say I don't read graphic novels and comics that come my way, but I don't seek them out as much as I used to. I wouldn't know where to start. I recently did an essay on Hillary Chute's study *Disaster Drawn*, about war and trauma in graphic narratives. A brilliant book.

I'd love to work with Paul on another project—he's extraordinarily knowledgeable about comics, in addition to being a great writer. And he's a blast to work with. We made a good team.

Hard Light *features an ancient device, a sort of primitive stone flip-comic. I'm assuming, perhaps naively, that you didn't make it up. Do you have one?*

No, I didn't make it up—I wish I had! It's called a thaumatrope, and I remember seeing one when I was a kid. Basically you draw a picture on both sides of a big button or a round piece of cardboard—almost the same image, but with a slight change, the way you make a flipbook. You add a hole (or sometimes two), thread a piece of string through, then wind it up on the string. When the string unwinds, the thaumatrope spins. The images flicker, and your eye and brain register them as a single image that's moving, like a simple animation. It's a very basic example of the persistence of vision.

At the British Museum a few years ago, I saw an amazing exhibit of Ice Age art, stuff from all over Europe. And there was a little thaumatrope, a bone disc with a bison carved on each side and a hole drilled through the middle. On one side it's a young bison, a calf; on the other side it's an adult. So when you thread it and spin it, you see the bison go from young to old and back again, over and over.

An image of fecundity? Of death?

When it was found many years ago, scientists assumed it was a button. Then someone (probably some scientist's kid) added a string, spun it—and thus was (re)discovered the thaumatrope, Ice Age animation technology.

Only three or four of these have ever been found. In one, a man with a spear is menacing a cave bear; on the other side, he's flat on his ass and the cave bear is menacing *him*. It's like a prehistoric cartoon!

So thaumatropes are very real, if very rare.

I did make one for myself when I was working on *Hard Light*. Cardboard, of course, but it works. Inspired, I "made up" an ancient camera obscura for the novel. I'm still waiting for some anthropologist to dig up a real one somewhere.

You seem to me to be a regional novelist, in a way, but your region can be hard to locate. Where is Bohemia today?

Bohemia is a floating world, a moveable feast—it's anywhere you have creative people who form their own world and their own alliances, relatively free of the overlords of our consumer society. It may be tough to find, but it's there.

My Jeopardy *item. You provide the question after I provide the answer: They function as air bags for careless readers.*

Trigger warnings. Amazon reviews. Spoiler alerts.

I know, that's three answers. That's why I'm not on *Jeopardy.*

Did you go to SF & Fantasy conventions before you were a published pro? Who were the first people you met in the field?

I'd published one story when I went to my first SF con, which was Disclave, in 1988. At the time I was taking a writing workshop at the Writer's Center in Bethesda with Richard Grant, who became my partner for some years (and is my kids' father). Richard had introduced me to Steve Brown, the editor of the influential SF magazine *Science Fiction Eye*, which was where my first reviews and critical essays appeared. Both of them encouraged me to go to Disclave, so I did.

It was a game changer for me. I met Mike Dirda there, who was an editor and critic at the *Washington Post Book World* (he went on to win the Pulitzer Prize a few years later), and he became a good friend. Mike asked if I'd like to do a book review, and of course I said yes. So that was the start of my career as a reviewer. You don't become rich from writing book reviews, but I've always loved it, and Mike gave me that break.

A few months later, I went to my first Worldcon, again with Steve Brown and also with Paul Witcover, who's been one of my closest friends since 1981. I met a number of writers and editors there, some of whom became good friends. I also met my agent, who I've been with ever since.

I always encourage aspiring writers to go to conventions. The infamous bank robber Willie Sutton was once asked by a judge, "Why do you keep robbing banks?" Willie replied, "Because that's where they keep the money." Cons are where they keep the writers and editors and agents and readers.

You once claimed I helped give you a start in doing novelizations and tie-ins. I apologize for that. Are you still doing that sort of thing?

That was one of the best things that ever happened to me! It gave me a chance to work another part of my writing brain, and it taught me how to work fast. I've always been very grateful for that.

I especially loved doing the Boba Fett juveniles for Scholastic—they were fun to write, and the Lucasfilm people were wonderful to work with. And I got the best fan mail ever ("You are my favorite writer in the whole world!") from little boys who had just read their first book.

As for doing another tie-in, I did stop doing novelizations a few years ago. But never say never, right? I'm a working writer, which means a lot of financial insecurity. I try not to turn down work, though I do want to focus on my own writing more than, say, any forthcoming Catwoman adaptations.

What did you think of that stupid movie about Thomas Wolfe and Maxwell Perkins, Genius*?*

I didn't see it, but I want to! I love bad movies about artists and writers. *Total Eclipse*, about Rimbaud and Verlaine, was silly, though David Thewlis had a great turn as Verlaine. I've seen it twice. *Fur*, with Nicole Kidman as Diane Arbus, was also pretty bad. Can't wait to see it again.

I think that John Waters should have right of first refusal on any biopic about a famous writer or artist.

You were into ecclesiastical terror long before Dan Brown. I'm thinking of the Benandanti in Waking the Moon. *Did you assemble that dark adversary from life or literature?*

From both. The Benandanti were a real group of people in medieval and early Renaissance Italy. I first came across them in *Ecstasies: Deciphering the Witches' Sabbath*, by the Italian historian Carlo Ginzburg, one of the best and most influential books I've ever read. I obviously embroidered on the real Benandanti for my own fell purposes in *Waking the Moon* and *Black Light*. Balthazar Warnick, my Benandante character, has made cameos in other books of mine.

Paul Park and John Crowley have also featured the Benandanti in their work, in very different ways. They're kind of an all-purpose secret ancient cult.

Do you have a drill for writing? You know: the where and the when, the cat, the coffee, the lucky pajamas, etc.

No. I mostly follow Mickey Spillane's advice: "Get your ass in a chair." I feel like I do my best writing at Tooley Cottage, which is my office, but I've written in hotel rooms, my parents' house, the British Library, and various other libraries. But not coffee shops or public places like that. I don't like writing in public, except in journals, or note-taking.

I don't have much of a special routine, though I do have a few songs I listen to, to psych myself up—"Valentine" by the Replacements, which I've used since first hearing it in 1987, and "Dice Behind Your Shades" by the Mats' frontman Paul Westerberg. And Neil Young's haunting "Pocahontas," which for me is Cass Neary's theme song. It gets at something so primal and rage-filled and true and sad about America, about loss and disenfranchisement. I know it's about our country's indigenous people, and Cass isn't Native American. But for whatever reason, that's the one song that immediately puts me in her head, and has since I started writing *Generation Loss* a dozen years ago.

What did you think of that great Swedish vampire movie, Let the Right One In*?*

I loved it. What an incredible story, what an incredible film, what a beautiful sad ending. The U.S. remake wasn't terrible, just totally unnecessary.

It was *terrible, but let's move on. Where do you write? Do you have a separate office? Is there a window over your desk? If you cleaned it, what would you see?*

I'm very lucky in that I have a beautiful, tiny cottage that I use as an office. I bought it in 1990, when it was a derelict little fishing camp, a few weeks before my first child was born. We lived there, without running water or indoor plumbing, for eight years, before buying a "real" house a few miles away.

It was tight quarters, three hundred square feet when I bought it, four hundred square feet now. I raised two kids there (my son was born two years after we moved in), and for many years it was a work in progress.

I hired friends to do the renovation and new construction. A boatbuilder friend once told me that if I thought about Tooley Cottage as a house, it was a very small house, but if I thought of it as a boat, it would be a good-sized boat. That was helpful.

Now it's beautiful, though it's still tiny. I love it more than anything except for my family and friends. It's on a lake, with a large wetland, so there's lots of wildlife—moose, beavers, otters, foxes, bobcats, mink, deer, bald eagles, osprey, blue herons, kingfishers, turtles, snakes, fishers, all kinds of migratory waterfowl and fish and amphibians. Once when the kids were little we saw a wolf—it was killed a few weeks later up in Ellsworth. Flying squirrels live in the rafters, which I know isn't good for the house, but still—flying squirrels!

It's also a mosquito and black fly preserve—it can be very buggy, because of the wetland. The window *is* kind of grubby, but it looks onto the water, which is only a stone's-throw away. It's a magical place, kind of a cross between Bag End and Merlyn's cottage in *The Sword in the Stone.*

But the truth is, when I'm working I hardly ever look out the window. I have to remind myself every few hours to stand up and go outside and look around. Sometimes I'm shocked to see where I am.

Do you read poetry for fun? What poets do you hate?

I do read poetry for fun, though I tend to return to the poets I've already read—Cavafy, Auden, Rimbaud, Bishop, Anne Carson, Anthony Hecht, Geoffrey Hill, Roethke, Eavan Boland, Yeats, Sappho . . .

I love poetry but I couldn't write it if my life depended on it. Maybe that's why.

Some of my teaching colleagues are poets, like T Fleischmann and Brandon Som and Jeanne Marie Beaumont, and I love both reading their work and hearing them read it aloud. I like Billy Collins. He wrote a funny poem about a mouse discovering fire that I reread every year.

Of course there's a poet I hate—this awful Christian poet we were forced to read in parochial school. I won't tell you his name because I don't want to go to Hell.

You write beautifully. That can be an impediment for some authors. How have you managed to make (and keep) it an asset?

There's a definitely a danger in writing pretty, precious prose, and I've been guilty of it, especially early in my career. I'm probably still guilty of it, on occasion, though I hope not as much as I was twenty-odd years ago.

I like to try different things when I write. When I wrote *Generation Loss*, I did so with the intent of working in the noir mode, something I'd never done before. Very stripped-down, terse, often dialogue-heavy prose. I hated writing that novel—there was a huge learning curve—and while I can't say I've mastered that voice, I think I've learned how to do it better.

With *Wylding Hall*, I wanted it to read like an oral history, so I created a series of fictional interviews with musicians, which was very constraining but also fun, maybe more like writing a play than a novel.

I still love to write lyrically, and in some ways that might be my more natural voice. But just because you can do something well doesn't mean you should do it all the damn time. Just because you know the right answer in class, you shouldn't always be the one to shout it out. Sometimes it's a good idea to keep your mouth shut. So sometimes I try to turn off the "lyrical" part of my brain and let a little breathing room into the narrative for another voice to speak.

Maine has one other famous writer, Sarah Orne Jewett. Have you read her work? Has Stephen King?

I read *The Country of the Pointed Firs* years ago and really enjoyed it. Her work holds up well. There's definitely something old-fashioned about it, but her depictions of Mainers and Maine are on the money. I know some folks who'd fit into one of her small towns even today.

I doubt that you get line edited severely. But I could be wrong. Am I?

No, you're right. I don't get a lot of line editing—I tend to edit my own work ruthlessly, and revise over and over and over again. I'd keep revising it once it hits the bookstores if I could.

What kind of car do you drive? I ask this of everyone.

A 2002 Subaru Outback with 241,000 miles on it. Part of it is held together with duct tape. I should send you a photo. It works really well. We also have a 2002 Volvo wagon that I inherited from my daughter when she moved to Maui a year ago. It has about 150,000 miles on it. It looks nicer than the Subaru, but the A/C doesn't work. In the olden days, you didn't need air conditioning in Maine, but with climate change you do.

I've never owned a new car. It just seems wrong.

What's that knocking noise from the attic?

Sarah Orne Jewett and Stephen King, duking it out.

The Woman Men Didn't See

HERE IS THE SADDEST story I have ever heard: the story of a woman tragically born a half-century too soon.

Alice Sheldon was brilliant, accomplished, beautiful, affluent. Her 1920s childhood experiences in the African wilderness were the stuff of fever dreams; as a teen debutante in Chicago, she could have been played by Katharine Hepburn, though one thinks Frances Farmer might have brought more to the role. Sheldon's subsequent careers—as a WAC, as a CIA intelligence officer, as a psychologist—were overshadowed by her mother's long and successful stint as a writer, as well as by bouts of mental illness and Alice's profound unease with her own sexual identity.

For fifty years this volatile psychic amalgam simmered, with a few added ingredients tossed in—a violent early marriage, long-term amphetamine dependence, a bipolar mood disorder, binge drinking, unhappy love affairs with men, faltering attempts to become a serious painter and writer, even a turn as a chicken farmer in rural New Jersey—until, in 1967, Alice Sheldon finally achieved the creative alchemy she'd been striving for, and the science fiction writer James Tiptree Jr. was born.

One often reads of biographies that their subjects could be fictional characters. It's safe to say that the life of Alice Sheldon (brilliantly dealt with in Julia Phillips' *James Tiptree, Jr.: The Double Life of Alice B. Sheldon*, winner of the National Book Award) would defy even the most extravagant novelistic imagination. Artist, CIA operative, gender-bending literary seductress with a Hemingwayesque alter-ego, Sheldon ensured there'd be no Hollywood ending when, in a suicide pact, she murdered her elderly husband, then shot herself in their suburban home. As Dave Barry says, I am not making this up: Who would fall for it?

But a lot of people did fall for Sheldon's literary persona, most famously Robert Silverberg, one of SF's most respected authors, who wrote in his 1975 introduction to Tiptree's collection *Warm Worlds and Otherwise*: "It has been suggested that Tiptree is female, a theory that I find absurd, for there is to me something ineluctably masculine about Tiptree's writing. I don't think the novels of Jane Austen could have been written by a man nor the stories of Ernest Hemingway by a woman, and in the same way I believe the author of the James Tiptree stories is male."

Well, few things are ineluctably masculine in our era, and Silverberg certainly has nothing to be ashamed of. Tiptree fooled all of the writers and editors he corresponded with during the heady years he was writing his best work, from 1967 until November 1976, when Sheldon discovered this letter in Tiptree's P.O. Box:

> Dear Tip,
> Okay, I'm going to lay all my cards on the table. You are not required to do likewise. You've probably heard from people already, but word is spreading very fast that your true name is Alice Sheldon. . . .

For someone who had built and dismantled an often shaky professional and sexual identity untold times over the years, before finding success and acceptance among the community of science fiction writers, editors, and fans, this note (from Tiptree's correspondent Jeff Smith) must have echoed like a tocsin, an alarm. The cat was, finally, out of the bag. The ineluctably masculine science fiction writer James Tiptree Jr. was in fact a bridge-playing, sixty-something suburban matron who lived with her retired husband in McLean, Virginia.

Alice Hastings Bradley was born in 1915. Her father, Herbert Bradley, made his fortune in real estate. Her mother, Mary Hastings Bradley, was in her lifetime a well-known writer, author of books like *The Innocent Adventuress* and *The Wine of Astonishment*—"a socialite, an explorer, and a big game hunter," according to biographer Philips, "[whose] earnings kept her daughter in mink coats and finishing schools." Alice and her parents lived in an expansive top-floor apartment near Lake Michigan that included a penthouse and roof garden, as well as a cook, a chauffeur, and a series of governesses.

Alice's mother, Mary, comes across as the sort of writer whose career and ego depended, to some extent, on her family and friends acting as supporting players in the continuing drama of her life. In 1921, Mary took her show on the road: she enlisted herself, Herbert, and six-year-old Alice as safari companions to the naturalist and big-game hunter Carl Akeley, whose glass-eyed trophies still gaze at viewers from dioramas in the Field Museum of Chicago and the American Museum of Natural History in Manhattan.

Alice's adventures were later recounted by her mother in several cheerful children's travelogues, *Alice in Jungleland*, *Alice in Elephantland*, and *Trailing the Tiger*. Alice's own experience seems more problematic, if not downright traumatic. The group shot and slaughtered an elephant, which was eaten by villagers. The next day their African porters went off to hunt, returning with a prisoner they claimed had attacked them. Philips describes the aftermath: "That night the Bradleys heard screams, and in the morning the man was gone. . . . One of the 'boys' told them he had been killed and eaten. . . . Alice lay awake and heard the whole thing."

Among other adventures, Alice's mother jokingly offered her blonde daughter in trade for a chief's ivory bracelet, and Alice witnessed a group of Batwa pygmies dancing and wondered, "Am I a Batwa? I'm little." It's almost anticlimactic to add that her mother shot and killed a lion, or that the formaldehyde-soaked remains of a young gorilla speared by one of Akeley's guides were stored beneath Alice's cot.

"It was early impressed on me that I was viable only within the sheltering adult group," the adult Alice wrote; "that the outside was dangerous and beyond my strength. . . . I never was allowed to learn to combat it; I lived helplessly inside . . . wondering how I could meet each horrible challenge, and never getting a chance to practice."

This is a long way from the child described in her mother's book as "dancing along at the head of the line [of porters], holding her Daddy's or Mummy's hand and waving a greeting to the native women in the fields."

The Bradleys returned to Chicago in 1922 but two years later went back to Africa, this time exploring the Ituri Rainforest. Nine-year-old Alice, despite her pleas, was forbidden a gun, though she did have an "old-fashioned crinoline" for costume parties. As they traveled into the rainforest, they often found themselves the first white people the villagers had ever encountered, and, as biographer Phillips observes, "experienced what for most science fiction writers is only a story or a metaphor: first contact." Alice entertained villagers by demonstrating how a door opened and closed, and showed them how her doll's blue-glass eyes would do the same. She saw lepers and heard of the ritual mutilation of girls' genitals, which "scared my immature soul sick." Most horrifying of all, she came upon the naked corpses of two men who had been "Stripped, tortured, tied to posts, and left to perish in the sun." There was no place for this event in any of Mary Bradley's published travelogues, but she and her husband took photographs, and there was no way their impressionable, sensitive daughter could have forgotten it: "You think of a crucifixion as taking place on well-edged beams, straight from the wood polisher. No such thing."

On their return, the Bradleys stopped in Calcutta, where, Alice later wrote, "we'd step over dying people with dying babies in their arms . . . a man on the steps of the Ganges reverently—and quite inadequately—burning his mother's body, and then leaping into the water to fish up the still recognizable skull and pry out the gold teeth."

These were the events that shaped Alice Sheldon from early childhood, exposing the rift between the beloved, spoiled daughter of American upper-middle-class privilege and the world she was thrust into, where a child could stumble onto the rotting corpses of men who had been tortured to death, but it was considered inappropriate for a girl to carry a gun, even a toy weapon that might have given her some sense of control over the whirling chaos around her.

The Alice Sheldon who emerges from Philips' biography and her own later journals often demonstrates the disassociativeness found in individuals with multiple personality disorders—"To grow up as a girl is . . . to be reacted to as nothing or as a thing—and nearly to become that thing"—as well as a grim sense of the worst that humanity can do—"Auschwitz—My Lai—etc. etc. etc. did not surprise me one bit, later on."

As a teenager at private school she suffered the solitude, sometimes self-imposed, of the extremely gifted, and had migraines severe enough that she would bang her head against the walls of the girl's bathroom, "to try to 'break' whatever was hurting so inside." Later, at boarding school in Switzerland, she would stand too close to the rails as trains barreled past, and made at least one suicide attempt, when she slashed her wrists with a razor. She developed intense crushes on other girls, and had a few same-sex sexual interludes (kissing, fondling); but she was never able to integrate Desire into a romantic relationship with another woman.

"All forms of sex should be explored," she wrote at twenty-four, "and many games should be learned. Relations with other people should be violent and experimental, with the idea of developing a mask to prevent erosion of the personality by other personalities."

The developing of that mask took up much of Alice Sheldon's life. Throughout much of her life, she was a woman in extremis, but one who remained very much her mother's daughter when it came to keeping a stiff upper lip, no matter the cost. As an adult (and eerily prefiguring the title of one of her best-known stories, "Love Is the Plan, the Plan Is Death"), Alice told her mother, "You 'taught' me, without meaning to, that love is the prelude to appalling pain." A bizarre brush with mother-daughter incest when Alice was fourteen can only have added to her sense that lesbianism was something monstrous.

Yet pain must somehow be endured, and for decades Sheldon did so with grace and wit and what can only be described as valor. Nine days after her December 20 debut, at eighteen, she eloped with a boy she'd met at a Christmas Eve dance, a Princeton student and aspiring novelist named William Davey. The marriage lasted six years, and in terms of spectacular dysfunction (drinking, drugging, visiting brothels) seems second only to that of William Burroughs and his common-law wife, Joan Vollmer. As Alice put it, "Anyone who shoots a real gun at you when drunk and angry is simply not husband material, regardless of his taste in literature."

Bill Davey encouraged his beautiful wife to paint, but their sexual relationship was a disaster. She had affairs with men, all apparently unsatisfying. Years later she confided to

Joanna Russ, "I am (was) notoriously fucked up about sex." She wrote with austere detachment that "to paint that which one wishes to be seized by, etc., is a sort of contradiction"; yet she also wrote (drunkenly, biographer Phillips suggests) in an otherwise empty sketchbook about her need to "ram myself into a crazy soft woman and come, come, spend, come, make her pregnant Jesus to be a man . . . I love women I will never be happy."

Still, Alice soldiered on. She divorced Bill Davey in 1941, moved back in with her parents and got a job as an art critic for the *Chicago Sun*. Despite her continuing attraction toward women, she dated men and in 1942 enlisted in the Women's Army Auxiliary Corps (later the Women's Army Corps). In her early days as a WAC in basic training, Alice experienced a near-ecstatic experience of living in a women's utopia. "Women seen for the first time at ease, unselfconscious, swaggering or thoughtful, sizing everything up openly, businesslike, all personalities all unbending and unafraid."

Her rapture faded quickly, ending in a bang-out fight with another, stronger, woman (a physical education teacher) whom Alice nearly strangled—an event she later recalled as an experience when she "felt fully alive." It's tempting to see in this signal occurrence at Fort Des Moines the first mad glimmer of James Tiptree himself, wrestling with the demonic Female Other until pulled away by several intervening women officers.

When the war ended, Captain Alice Davey was stationed in London as a Pentagon photo-interpreter. There she met Colonel Huntington "Ting" Sheldon, "a tall, graying, gracious senior officer, formerly of Yale and Wall Street." Captain Davey "challenged Colonel Sheldon to a game of chess," says Philips, "played blindfolded, and won. He fell in love."

Alice summed up their sexual relationship thus: "Him and women: Had to get drunk—then of course impotent." Despite (or because of) this, they married, and returned to the U.S. early in 1946. Her relentless self-invention continued through the next two decades, as she became a housewife, chicken farmer, CIA analyst, and graduate student at George Washington University in DC, eventually earning a doctorate in psychology by studying how rats react to novel stimuli and experiences. She also wrote, trying to follow up the success of a story that appeared in *The New Yorker* in 1946, but none of her ambitious projects came to fruition.

And she read—science fiction and fantasy, a love since childhood when she first encountered *Weird Tales* magazine and now a necessary escape valve from her observations of rats and her dissertation-writing binges, fueled by speed and alcohol and her own manic energy.

And over the next decade, her beloved childhood literature was changing: it was no longer wholly dependent on the bug-eyed monsters and rocket jockeys of pulp's Golden Age. Writers like Kurt Vonnegut, Harlan Ellison, Philip K. Dick, J.G. Ballard, Thomas M. Disch, Samuel R. Delany, Joanna Russ, and Ursula K. Le Guin tackled gender and environmental and social issues that reflected the sweeping changes and excesses of the 1960s. Their prose style, often as overheated as that of their pulp forebears, drew on the burgeoning drug culture. So did the images of psychic and/or sexual disintegration that swirled around the works of Dick, Russ, and Delany in particular. For Alice Sheldon, reading their stories in the pages of *Analog* and *Astounding* and *Galaxy*, it must have seemed like a Mad Tea Party she was fated to join.

According to Philips, "The stories started coming to her when she was writing up her dissertation, studying for her orals, skimping on sleep, and using as much Dexedrine as she dared. . . . Sometime in the spring of 1967, Alice Sheldon, a fifty-one-year-old research psychologist, typed them up and sent them out to science fiction magazines."

The pseudonym she chose was deliberately outrageous: James Tiptree Jr. The surname was taken from a jar of jam on a supermarket shelf, though critic John Clute suggests the nickname "Tip" derived from Princess Ozma's androgynous counterpart, Tip, in L. Frank Baum's Oz books, which Alice Sheldon had read. The first stories went out not long after she received her doctorate, in February 1967. What happened next is the stuff of literary legend, though in fact Tiptree collected several rejection letters, including one from legendary SF editor John W. Campbell, who grumbled, "One of the troubles with a majority of modern stories is that nowadays the idea of an heroic Hero is considered gauche or something."

But that fall Campbell bought one story for *Analog*, Harry Harrison took a second for *Fantastic*, and Frederik Pohl accepted a third (which Campbell had already rejected), for *If*. James Tiptree Jr. had achieved escape velocity.

His first SF story, "Birth of a Salesman," appeared in the March 1968 *Analog*. That same year Tiptree sold three more stories, but it was the appearance of "The Last Flight of Dr. Ain" in *Galaxy* a year later that established the tone of Tiptree's best work, the literary equivalent of an ice shard to the heart: chilly, razor-sharp, and terrifying. Tiptree's grim, deliberate account of a doctor unleashing a deadly virus on humankind via air travel—appropriated years later by Terry Gilliam in his film *12 Monkeys*—was only 2,500 words long. Yet her writing here showed the assassin's gifts she was to utilize in her best work: deadly grace and concision and a certain heartlessness, joined to a narrative that never pauses to take a breath. If one were to take a Freudian view of Sheldon's life and work, it's all here in the stories that followed. Sexual repression and self-restraint exploded into a maenad's frenzy of destruction, wreaked upon individuals and urges that control and despoil the world—men, scientists, the blind biological thrust toward sexual union; a clinically ruthless biodeterminism whose ultimate goal was extinction.

The stories, of course, are what really matter about Tiptree. Sheldon's greatest work—"Dr. Ain," "The Girl Who Was Plugged In," "The Women Men Don't See," "Love Is the Plan, the Plan Is Death," "The Scientist Who Wouldn't Do Awful Things to Rats," and, especially, "The Screwfly Solution," one of the most frightening stories ever written, penned under Sheldon's other nom de plume, Raccoona Sheldon—stands among the best short fiction of the late twentieth century. It's a body of work that has never received its due from mainstream critics.

Sheldon's life in the late 1960s and early 1970s reads like an SF version of *Catch Me If You Can*, with her masculine alter-ego creating and maintaining a voluminous correspondence, a Real Guy among predominately Real Guy Writers. The list of

Tiptree's correspondents is a roll call of those who were part of the incredible efflorescence that was American science fiction in the 1970s: Ursula Le Guin, Joanna Russ, Damon Knight, Phil Dick, Harlan Ellison, Barry Malzberg, David Gerrold, Ted White, Charles Platt, Vonda McIntrye—you get the idea. Tiptree flirted with Russ and Le Guin, but he showed his manlier face to his male friends, coming off as a bluff guy's guy—but soft enough for a woman.

Too soft, maybe. As curiosity about Tiptree grew in the SF community, gossip spread about the secretive author. Tip was a spy, a spook; he was crazy; he was a woman. This last could still be a liability, as indicated in a letter from Harry Harrison demanding rewrites: "I think 'big shimmery' on page 26 too purple. Or girl-writer term or something." Tiptree's fear of being outed as a girl writer must have been acute. A 1972 letter to Harrison has the undeniable edge of hysteria.

"WILL YOU LAY OFF? . . . Harry, listen. You've been a great friend and I value it more than I can say. My life is a mixed-up mess right now. I have personal problems like other people have termites. I'm barely viable. You and my other friends in the sf world, and the writing, are all that's keeping me sane."

Biographer Phillips says that Harrison recoiled from this letter, thinking, "This guy's on a twist." Later, after Sheldon's identity was revealed, Harrison concluded that his friend had not been "nuts" but "a woman who was just being very female about it."

It's a comment that underscores the blatant misogyny of the time, and also of people in the field—writers, editors, most of them men—who should have known better. Why is behavior that would be considered "nuts" for a man considered normal for a female? This is the crux of Alice Sheldon's often tormented life, the disconnect between her projected voice—her stories—and her everyday self. She sometimes seems like a prime candidate for gender-reassignment therapy; at other times, a lesbian so deeply closeted that one's instinct is to drag her into daylight and shout, "See? IT'S NOT SO BAD AFTER ALL."

But it was bad, after all. Today, with the Internet, Sheldon's cover would probably be blown in a matter of days or weeks. She certainly appears to have been courting disclosure with her adoption of a second, female, even more transparent pseudonym, the absurd Raccoona Sheldon, who in a dizzying coup-des-lettres carried on her own correspondence with various SF figures. As it was, Jeff Smith's letter to P.O. Box 315 arrived on November 23, 1976, and James Tiptree Jr.'s identity unraveled over the following months. So, tragically, did his writing career. Alice Sheldon continued to publish after the revelation that he was a she, but her best work was done.

Gardner Dozois—an editor who was not a misogynist, then or now—threw down the gauntlet by asking, "Where in your fiction are the equally convincing portraits of what it's like to be a girl growing up? . . . It wouldn't surprise me at all to find that 'Tiptree's' best work is yet to come."

Sheldon responded that she "is maybe a mad woman, maybe an ex-good-researcher, but is not a science fiction or any other kind of writer. I am nothing." Two years later, in 1978, she threw all her new work—notes, novel, stories—into the woodstove, and told Ursula Le Guin, "I am trying to become nothing."

Sheldon's great tragedy was that she could not seize her power to write as herself. The masks that she spent a lifetime creating could not, in the end, hide what she really was and what she loved. When, post-Tiptree, Joanna Russ penned her a personal love letter, Sheldon replied, "Oh, had 65 years been different! I like some men a lot, but from the start, before I knew anything, it was always girls and women who lit me up."

Alice Sheldon and Joanna Russ never met. This was not merely a failure of nerve on Sheldon's part. It was a failure of self. All her life she wrote of being attracted to aliens, the other (she developed a passionate crush on Leonard Nimoy's Spock); but the truth was that the alien was unquestionably not other, but her own kind. Faced with the image of desire in the mirror, she felt compelled to shatter it. No reasoned discussion of Tiptree's work or of Sheldon's complicated inner life can quite prepare you for Sheldon's statement that "My 'illness' has taken the form of writing some more science-fiction stories. . . . I am going to finish the series with one about a man who kills EVERYBODY, that will make me feel better."

Nor does it prepare a reader for what she will feel the first time she encounters "The Screwfly Solution" or "The Last Voyage of Dr. Ain" or "The Women Men Don't See"—the same emotion, perhaps, that gripped that physical education teacher in Fort Des Moines, or Alice Sheldon's husband when he realized, as Phillips suggests, that his wife was going to kill him: pure fear. In the end, Alice Sheldon really was the woman nobody saw.

Tom Disch

FEW PEOPLE MAKE A successful career of contemplating death and suicide; fewer still approach the subject with the genuine ebullience and elegant despair of the prolific, criminally underappreciated writer Thomas M. Disch, who shot himself in his Union Square apartment, in New York, on the Fourth of July, 2008.

Disch was a seminal figure in science fiction's New Wave, the iconoclastic 1960s movement that gave the genre a literary pedigree and popularized the term "speculative fiction." His books influenced writers such as William Gibson and Jonathan Lethem; his dystopias *Camp Concentration* and *334* are considered science fiction classics, along with his greatest novel, *On Wings of Song*, a beautiful, dark meditation on the power and limits of transcendence through art.

An openly gay man for most of his working life, Disch wrote mysteries, historical novels and neo-gothic satires; children's books, including *The Brave Little Toaster* and its sequel; at least five collections of short fiction; fifteen volumes of poetry, always as Tom Disch; plays and libretti; four volumes of nonfiction; screen adaptations, novelizations, and one of the first interactive computer games. He edited anthologies; he wrote book reviews, theater reviews, art reviews, music reviews. He wrote collaboratively and pseudonymously; he kept a popular blog, *Endzone*, in which he shared new poems, some unpleasant post-9/11 screeds, and witty discourses on the meaninglessness and minutiae of life. In his most recent novel, he wrote in the voice of God, and on his publisher's website answered questions from readers. He wrote and wrote and wrote and wrote, for the sheer joy of it and for an even more primal impulse: to tell a story to the dark.

"Storytelling is just absolutely natural to me. It's my way of getting along with people, I guess," he told an interviewer at the website Strange Horizons in 2001. He'd call friends and, after an exchange of pleasantries, ask, "May I read you something?" The answer was always yes and his voice would lift as he read a sonnet or villanelle, or perhaps the section from *The Word of God* where Disch's deity wonders whether His father was in fact Thomas Mann.

He had a wonderful speaking voice, fluid and seductive. He sounded like John Malkovich, and he looked a bit like Malkovich too, in his prime. I grew up reading Disch's work, starting with "The Roaches" as a twelve-year-old and devouring the novels as I got older. I first met him casually in the late 1980s but only got to know him and his partner, poet Charles Naylor, during their last years—far too brief a time. Tall and physically imposing, in public Disch could project a slightly threatening aloofness, with his shaved head, impressive tattoos, bodybuilder's mass. The silken voice that emerged from that intimidating form made him seem even more dangerous, one of those wizards who is subtle and quick to anger.

But then he'd dissolve in laughter and it would all suddenly seem to be a pose, a disguise, part of a vast elaborate joke that you were in on—maybe. He could be irascible, scathingly dismissive; he held grudges and burned bridges. In recent years he'd put on weight, which exacerbated other problems: diabetes, sciatica, neuropathy, depression. He had difficulty walking and was almost housebound.

And since the turn of the millennium he'd endured a Job-like succession of personal tragedies, beginning with a fire that severely damaged the Union Square apartment he shared with Naylor, his partner of thirty years; frozen pipes that caused a mold infestation at his house in Barryville, NY; Naylor's long illness and eventual death from colon cancer; and, finally, eviction proceedings begun by the landlord almost immediately after Naylor's death.

During this siege Disch struggled with crushing grief and depression—only a real deity would not—yet he also had a humorous resignation that seemed very close to valor. He once said, "I am certainly a 'death of God' writer," and much of his work seems fueled by the rage and sense of betrayal of a former believer, as well as a refined sense of the ridiculousness of religious institutions, and the ultimate, absurd realization that we all die alone. His best work builds on Eugène Ionesco's dictum: "We are made to be immortal, and yet we die. It's horrible, it can't be taken seriously."

Death was the subject Disch returned to again and again, in his fiction and his poetry. Sometimes it was murder, spurred by passion or twisted religious or political fervor. Sometimes, as in his early novel *The Genocides*, or his later satirical novel *The Sub: A Study in Witchcraft*, it was simply a detached, clinical adjustment of the biological status quo, with untidy or unnecessary humans disposed of like irksome insects. He wrote often about suicide, nearly always without melodrama. "Laughter is just a slowed down scream of terror," he told Joseph Francavilla in a 1983 interview.

> . . . thoughtful minds are free of pain
> To the degree that they can think
> And alchemize their thoughts to ink.
> Happy the man who can declare
> His angst with any savoir faire.
> —Tom Disch, from "Waking New Year's Day, Without a Hangover," 1986

Born in Iowa in 1940, Disch spent his childhood and early teens in the Midwest before moving to New York, where he attended Cooper Union and New York University. He held the usual spate of desultory writers' jobs, most memorably a brief stint in *Swan Lake*'s corps de ballet, where he encouraged the other male dancers to sing "I am, I am, I am a swan" under their breath while Margot Fonteyn expired as Odette. In 1962 he wrote his first story in lieu of studying for an NYU exam and promptly sold it to the science fiction magazine *Fantastic*. He subsequently dropped out of school to devote himself to writing.

A number of beautifully crafted stories date from these early years. Among the best: "Descending," in which a man steps onto a department store elevator that only goes down, forever; the much-anthologized "The Roaches"; and the Kafkaesque "The Squirrel Cage," in which a writer works feverishly, endlessly, on a horror story he cannot even see, and which no one will ever read: "The story has gone on far too long. Nothing can be terrifying for years on end. I only *say* it's terrifying because, you know, I have to say something. Something or other. The only thing that could terrify me now is if someone were to come in. If they came in and said, 'All right, Disch, you can go now.' That, truly, would be terrifying."

In the mid-1960s he knocked around Europe and North Africa before touching down in London's Camden Town around 1967, where he became part of that moveable feast of Anglo-American writers and artists associated with the New Wave: Michael Moorcock, John and Judith Clute, John Sladek (a future Disch collaborator), Pamela Zoline, M. John Harrison.

The Genocides was published in 1965, a vision of Earth as an agribusiness run by extraterrestrials who sow the planet with a single vast plant crop, then methodically exterminate the human pests who infect their harvest. It ends badly. As Disch cheerfully pointed out in a 1979 interview published in the British journal *Foundation*, "Let's be honest, the real interest in this kind of story is to see some devastating cataclysm wipe mankind out. . . . My point was simply to write a book where you don't spoil that beauty and pleasure at the end."

His next major work, *Camp Concentration*, appeared in 1967 in *New Worlds*, the New Wave's flagship magazine, and a year later was published in book form. Now regarded as one of the greatest SF novels, at the time *Camp Concentration* was overshadowed by Daniel Keyes' *Flowers for Algernon*, which shared some themes and narrative structure. Inspired by the Faust legend, the novel unfolds as the journal of Louis Sacchetti, a schlubby poet interned at an American concentration camp for being a conscientious objector. There he and the other prisoners are injected with an experimental drug that boosts their intelligence even as it erodes their life span.

Samuel R. Delany wrote that *Camp Concentration* was "the first book within the SF field I have read for which my reaction was simple, total and complete envy: 'I wish I had written that.'" It remains in print and is probably Disch's best-known book, though Disch was dismissive of it in the 1979 *Foundation* interview: "I think it was probably not strong enough to stand on its own outside the genre. Not as a work of literature."

On Wings of Song, his 1979 masterpiece, is a work of literature. William Gibson called it "one of the great neglected masterpieces of late 20th-century science fiction"; Robert Drake named it part of "The Gay Canon." A savage, politically charged bildungsroman, the novel presents the American Midwest as a fundamentalist police state where air travelers are forced through security checkpoints, books and works of art are considered seditious, and Daniel Weinreb, a fourteen-year-old from Amesville, Iowa, is imprisoned for possession of copies of the *Minneapolis Star-Tribune*. After his release, he makes his way to Manhattan, a secular paradise, and struggles to become a bel canto singer.

The book's defining metaphor is a form of virtual reality that enables practitioners to experience ecstasy. Not everyone achieves this transcendence, and the attempt can be dangerous: disembodied souls, nicknamed "fairies," can be trapped and destroyed, their host bodies left in a vegetative state.

"Beauty is probably the antidote to evil—in practical terms for an artist," Disch once remarked. "Because art is one of the routes of access to joy, and joy is always problematical the moment it stops happening. You're always asking, 'Where is it? Why can't it be brought back?'" It was the essential question for Disch.

Later books explored the nature of evil in more satirical terms. Raised Catholic, Disch took the heretic's glee in attacking church hypocrisy in works like *The Priest: A Gothic Romance,* which featured pedophile clergy and murderous antiabortion protesters, and his play "The Cardinal Detoxes," which the Archdiocese of New York attempted to shut down. In Disch's version of Hell, the suicidal poet John Berryman is forced to haunt Minneapolis. He talked about writing a career guide for young girls titled "So You Want to Be the Pope"; the Supreme Being he channels in his final novel *The Word of God* is sensible and gossipy, as demonstrated by the answers He gives to readers on His publisher's website:

> Dearest God,
> Since food is the most recent topic: Why have you made the pit in avocados so infernally Large? And along the same lines, what's up with your pomegranate invention?
> —Norman

> Norman,
> You must have been kibbitzing with Proserpine. Her and her pomegranate diet. But as to avocado pits, your guess is as good as mine. But did you know you can grow whole avocado trees from those pits? It takes a lot of patience, but they will grow all the way to the ceiling if you let them.
> —God

Disch was an often brutal satirist who wrote a beloved children's book about sweet-natured household appliances, an ironist who would cheer up a visitor by reading aloud poems ostensibly penned by Paddington Bear, in Paddington's voice. He reveled in coincidence, in life and art. With Naylor, he wrote a marvelous historical novel, *Neighboring Lives*, that explored the web of connections between Victorian thinkers and artists in Pre-Raphaelite London. Naylor gave him joy; *On Wings of Song* was dedicated to him.

Almost exactly a year after Naylor's death in 2005, Disch began writing a sequence of poems, an extraordinary efflorescence of grief he shared on his blog. Eventually there were thirty-one of them. He titled the sequence "Winter Journey" after Schubert's lieder cycle *Winterreise* (a work Naylor loved). The poems are tragic, bitter, bleakly funny, romantic, heart-rending—and also accessible. You can hear him read them today on YouTube.

"The song does not end," Disch wrote in the closing pages of *On Wings of Song*, "and though he had written that song before he'd learned to fly himself, it was true. The moment one leaves one's body by the power of song, the lips fall silent, but the song goes on, and so long as one flies the song continues. He hoped, if he were to leave his body tonight, they would remember that. The song does not end."

Bibliography

Series

Winterlong

Winterlong (New York: Bantam Books, 1990)
Æstival Tide (New York: Bantam Books, 1992)
Icarus Descending (New York: Bantam Books, 1993)

Cass Neary

Generation Loss (Northampton, Massachusetts: Small Beer Press, 2007)
Available Dark (New York: St. Martin's Minotaur, 2012)
Hard Light (New York: St. Martin's Minotaur, 2016)

Individual Titles

Waking the Moon (London: HarperCollins, 1994)
Waking the Moon (New York: HarperPrism, 1995)
Glimmering (New York: HarperPrism, 1997)

Glimmering (Portland, OR: Underland Press, 2012)
Black Light (New York: HarperPrism, 1999)
Mortal Love (New York: HarperCollins/Morrow, 2004)
Radiant Days (New York: Viking, 2012)
Wylding Hall (Hornsea, East Yorkshire: PS Publishing, 2015)

Collections and Stories

Last Summer at Mars Hill (New York: HarperPrism, 1998)
Bibliomancy (Hornsea, East Yorkshire: PS Publishing, 2003)
Chip Crockett's Christmas Carol (Harold Wood, Essex: Beccon Publications, 2006)
Illyria (Hornsea, East Yorkshire: PS Publishing, 2006)
Saffron and Brimstone: Strange Stories (Milwaukie, OR: M Press, 2006)
Errantry: Strange Stories (Easthampton, Massachusetts: Small Beer Press, 2012)

Tie-ins

Star Wars

Star Wars: Boba Fett: Book 3: Maze of Deception (New York: Scholastic Paperbacks, 2003)
Star Wars: Boba Fett: Book 4: Hunted (New York: Scholastic Paperbacks, 2003)
Star Wars: Boba Fett: Book 5: A New Threat (New York: Scholastic Paperbacks, 2004)
Star Wars: Boba Fett: Book 6: Pursuit (New York: Scholastic Paperbacks, 2004)

Single Volumes

12 Monkeys (New York: HarperPrism, 1995)
Millennium: The Frenchman (New York: HarperPrism, 1997)
The X-Files: Fight the Future (New York: HarperPrism, 1998) with Chris Carter
Anna and the King (New York: Harper Paperbacks, 1999)
Catwoman (New York: Ballantine Books/Del Rey, 2004)
The Bride of Frankenstein: Pandora's Bride (Milwaukie, OR: Dark Horse Books, 2007)

About the Author

Elizabeth Hand is the bestselling author of fourteen novels and four collections of short fiction. Her work has received numerous awards, and several of her books have been *New York Times* and *Washington Post* Notable Books. Her recent, critically acclaimed novels featuring Cass Neary, "one of literature's great noir antiheroes," have been compared to those of Patricia Highsmith. She is a longtime critic and book reviewer whose work appears regularly in the *Los Angeles Times*, *Washington Post*, *Salon*, and the *Boston Review*, among many others. She teaches at the Stonecoast MFA program in creative writing and divides her time between the coast of Maine and North London.

Also available from PM Press

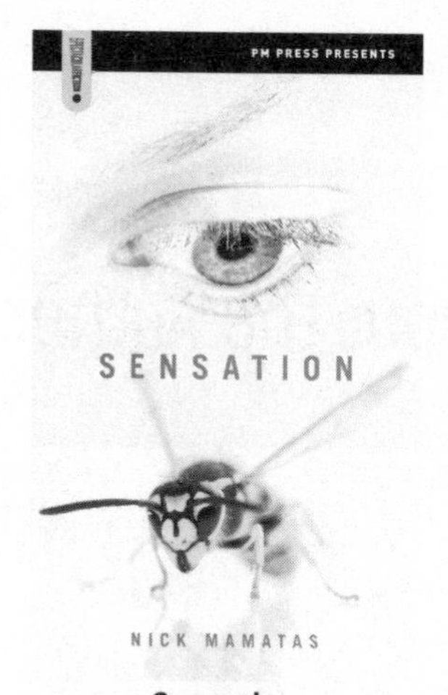

Sensation
Nick Mamatas
ISBN: 978-1-60486-354-3
$14.95

Damnificados
JJ Amaworo Wilson
ISBN: 978-1-62963-117-2
$15.95

Fire on the Mountain
Terry Bisson
Introduction by Mumia Abu-Jamal
ISBN: 978-1-60486-087-0
$15.95

Clandestine Occupations:
An Imaginary History
Diana Block
ISBN: 978-1-62963-121-9
$16.95

Also available from PM Press

Gypsy
Carter Scholz
ISBN: 978-1-62963-118-9
$13.00

The Great Big Beautiful Tomorrow
Cory Doctorow
ISBN: 978-1-60486-404-5
$12.00

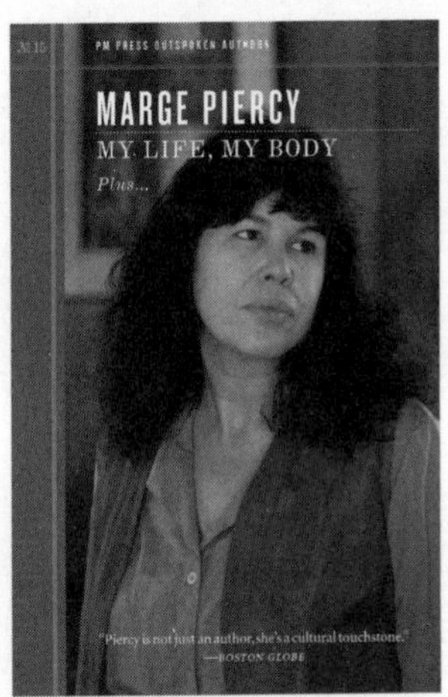

My Life, My Body
Marge Piercy
ISBN: 978-1-62963-105-9
$12.00

The Wild Girls
Ursula K. Le Guin
ISBN: 978-1-60486-403-8
$12.00

Also available from PM Press

Report from Planet Midnight

Nalo Hopkinson

ISBN: 978-1-60486-497-7

$12.00

The Science of Herself

Karen Joy Fowler

ISBN: 978-1-60486-825-8

$12.00

Raising Hell

Norman Spinrad

ISBN: 978-1-60486-810-4

$12.00

Patty Hearst & The Twinkie Murders: A Tale of Two Trials

Paul Krassner

ISBN: 978-1-629630-38-0

$12.00

Also available from PM Press

Mammoths of the Great Plains
Eleanor Arnason
ISBN: 978-1-60486-075-7
$12.00

New Taboos
John Shirley
ISBN: 978-1-60486-761-9
$12.00

Miracles Ain't What They Used to Be
Joe R. Lansdale
ISBN: 978-1-62963-152-3
$13.00

The Underbelly
Gary Phillips
ISBN: 978-1-60486-206-5
$14.00

Also available from PM Press

The Left Left Behind
Terry Bisson
ISBN: 978-1-60486-086-3
$12.00

The Lucky Strike
Kim Stanley Robinson
ISBN: 978-1-60486-085-6
$12.00

The Human Front
Ken MacLeod
ISBN: 978-1-60486-395-6
$12.00

Surfing the Gnarl
Rudy Rucker
ISBN: 978-1-60486-309-3
$12.00

FRIENDS OF PM

These are indisputably momentous times—the financial system is melting down globally and the Empire is stumbling. Now more than ever there is a vital need for radical ideas.

In the years since its founding—and on a mere shoestring—PM Press has risen to the formidable challenge of publishing and distributing knowledge and entertainment for the struggles ahead. With hundreds of releases to date, we have published an impressive and stimulating array of literature, art, music, politics, and culture. Using every available medium, we've succeeded in connecting those hungry for ideas and information to those putting them into practice.

Friends of PM allows you to directly help impact, amplify, and revitalize the discourse and actions of radical writers, filmmakers, and artists. It provides us with a stable foundation from which we can build upon our early successes and provides a much-needed subsidy for the materials that can't necessarily pay their own way. You can help make that happen—and receive every new title automatically delivered to your door once a month—by joining as a Friend of PM Press. And, we'll throw in a free T-shirt when you sign up.

Here are your options:

- $30 a month: Get all books and pamphlets plus 50% discount on all webstore purchases
- $40 a month: Get all PM Press releases (including CDs and DVDs) plus 50% discount on all webstore purchases
- $100 a month: Superstar—Everything plus PM merchandise, free downloads, and 50% discount on all webstore purchases

For those who can't afford $30 or more a month, we have Sustainer Rates at $15, $10, and $5. Sustainers get a free PM Press T-shirt and a 50% discount on all purchases from our website.

Your Visa or Mastercard will be billed once a month, until you tell us to stop. Or until our efforts succeed in bringing the revolution around. Or the financial meltdown of Capital makes plastic redundant. Whichever comes first.

PM Press was founded at the end of 2007 by a small collection of folks with decades of publishing, media, and organizing experience. PM Press co-conspirators have published and distributed hundreds of books, pamphlets, CDs, and DVDs. Members of PM have founded enduring book fairs, spearheaded victorious tenant organizing campaigns, and worked closely with bookstores, academic conferences, and even rock bands to deliver political and challenging ideas to all walks of life. We're old enough to know what we're doing and young enough to know what's at stake.

We seek to create radical and stimulating fiction and non-fiction books, pamphlets, t-shirts, visual and audio materials to entertain, educate, and inspire you. We aim to distribute these through every available channel with every available technology—whether that means you are seeing anarchist classics at our bookfair stalls; reading our latest vegan cookbook at the café; downloading geeky fiction e-books; or digging new music and timely videos from our website.

PM Press is always on the lookout for talented and skilled volunteers, artists, activists, and writers to work with. If you have a great idea for a project or can contribute in some way, please get in touch.

PM Press
PO Box 23912
Oakland CA 94623
510-658-3906
www.pmpress.org